"Did you attend a party last night?"

"A party," Sasha repeated.

"Yeah, one of those things where people get together and music is played. There's usually food and—"

"Jake, I know the definition of a party."

"Were you there, last night, wearing a reddish-blond curly wig, dressed like a tiger?" He thought he might be imagining discomfort where there was none. "Well, were you?"

"I know Lincoln and TJ asked you to look out for me. But seriously, you inquiring about my every move is not only unnecessary, it's becoming downright irritating."

"Does that mean you don't want to tell me where you were last night?"

"I was preparing to come here, to Point du Sable. Want to see my plane ticket?"

He raised a brow. "Do you have it on you?"

Sasha's expression made him laugh out loud.

She looked beyond him and waved. "Bye, Jake."

* * *

A Game of Secrets by Zuri Day is part of the The Eddington Heirs series.

Dear Reader,

Do you have a secret? Have you ever been sworn to keep one for somebody else? An unexpected, clandestine meeting leading to such a secret is the premise to Jake and Sasha's story. Sasha McDowell comes to Point du Sable from Washington, DC, to assist her godmother with a holiday event. She's excited at the prospect of seeing Jake Eddington, a childhood crush. Unfortunately—or fortunately, depending on who's asked—their first time together in a decade doesn't go the way either of them would have expected. What happens is a complete surprise, something that definitely shouldn't go public. That information getting out could have huge personal and professional ramifications. Not just for Jake and Sasha, but for their high-profile, influential families and the communities where each resides.

What do you think about having and keeping secrets? My family, especially the older members, pride themselves on being able to maintain privileged information. Those unable to do so are described as people who "can't hold water." I think that phrase has Southern origins but I don't know for sure. Just for the record, I can "hold water." Lots of it. So, feel free to tell me *all* your secrets, DayDreamers, at ZuriDay.com!

Zuri

ZURI DAY

——

A GAME OF SECRETS

Recycling programs for this product may not exist in your area.

ISBN-13: 978-1-335-58167-9

A Game of Secrets

Copyright © 2023 by Zuri Day

For questions and comments about the quality of this book, please contact us at CustomerService@Harlequin.com.

Harlequin Enterprises ULC
22 Adelaide St. West, 41st Floor
Toronto, Ontario M5H 4E3, Canada
www.Harlequin.com

Printed in U.S.A.

Zuri Day is the award-winning, nationally bestselling author of a slew of novels translated into almost a dozen languages. When not writing or enjoying the adventures of international travel, she can be found in the weeds—literally—engaged in gardening, her latest passion, or in the kitchen whipping up tasty vegan and vegetarian dishes while being a chef in her own mind! Check out her bookshelf and become a part of her beautiful day by signing up for her newsletter at ZuriDay.com.

Books by Zuri Day

Harlequin Desire

The Eddington Heirs

Inconvenient Attraction
The Nanny Game
Two Rivals, One Bed
A Game of Secrets

Sin City Secrets

Sin City Vows
Ready for the Rancher
Sin City Seduction
The Last Little Secret

Visit the Author Profile page
at Harlequin.com for more titles.

You can also find Zuri Day on Facebook,
along with other Harlequin Desire authors,
at Facebook.com/HarlequinDesireAuthors!

Keeping big secrets can lead to huge lies

Creative fabrications and false alibis

*The truth being revealed is the
price one must pay*

*While love sometimes justifies
the games people play.*

One

"Lone Ranger, or Zorro?"

Jake Eddington's body, clad in all black, physically responded to the intoxicating scent and sultry sound of a woman's voice so close that her damp breath tickled his earlobe. Jake loved the sound of women's voices. He loved their warm, damp spaces too. He was a connoisseur of all things female, voices in particular. That, along with natural butts and breasts and pretty eyes, like the pair that locked on him as he turned, immediately snaring him in their clutches. Brown with flecks of gold, they matched the woman's tiger costume, a tight mini and matching thigh-high boots that showed off delicate curves and came complete with ears, tail and a long, golden mane.

And a mask, of course.

"What do you think?" While asking the question, he tried to identify what little of the face he could see behind a mask that showed little more than lips and eyes. He'd grown up in nearby Point du Sable, the uberupscale community where many of the partygoers lived or had also grown up, and had been a regular on Chicago's elite party scene. In other words, he knew almost everybody. But what he could see of this femme fatale didn't look familiar at all.

Jake immediately made himself a promise to rectify that.

The woman tossed her curls to one side, her expression thoughtful. "Definitely Zorro," she concluded. "You don't strike me as the type of guy to spend much time alone."

A couple steps was all it took for Jake to invade the tigress's personal space. He took full advantage.

"And you are?"

He was close enough to catch another whiff of her perfume, a spicy, floral confection that beckoned him closer still. Another step placed his mouth close to her ear.

"Besides, of course, the most gorgeous feline I've ever encountered."

Her response as she leaned in and squeezed his forearm? A prolonged *purrrrr*.

Jake's mouth split into a smile. At the same time, his manhood jumped. He didn't recognize the voice or what he could see of the face. But so far, he liked her. A lot.

He repeated his attempt for personal info. "What's your name?"

"It's a masquerade party, so why would you ask?"

"Because it might be considered inappropriate to place a tantalizing kiss on the lips of a stranger."

"It might also be deemed wrong for me to slap an anonymous face, but that's what such an intrusion would cost you."

Spunky. I like that! He also decided those delicious-looking kissers were worth a punch. He thought it best not to tell her that.

Jake placed two big strong hands over his heart in mock wounded pride. "Ah, come on now. One of the reasons we wear masks at these things is for the freedom to give in to our...carnal desires. If you'd attended these before, you'd know that, so it must be your first time."

It was a clear attempt to find out more about her. She didn't take the bait. For Jake, that made her even more intriguing. He wouldn't exactly call himself promiscuous, but when not in a committed relationship, like now, he made the most of opportunities that presented themselves. In years past, these annual Halloween parties had gotten pretty wild. The later the hour and the more the alcohol flowed, it wasn't unusual to see partygoers in various states of undress, performing get-to-knows right on the dance floor. More than once, he'd opened one of the ten bedroom doors the mansion boasted to find it occupied. The only reason it hadn't happened to him was because of the lesson he'd learned—lock the door. Recent events had somewhat tempered the formerly carefree social scene, but he'd attended enough of his pro athlete clients' private parties to know that grown folk still liked to do what grown folk liked to do. Jake was cautious but he wasn't celibate. He wasn't stupid either. Less than ten minutes or ten feet into the party and he knew he was conversing with one of the most beautiful women in the house.

"Since your name is off-limits, what can I know about you?" His eyes swept over her costume, noting breasts that looked natural, a flat stomach and small waist. "That outfit alone tells me you're dangerous. Or at the very least up for adventure."

"Maybe."

"How can maybe become definitely? A couple turns on the dance floor? Sharing a plate of delicious hors d'oeuvres? There's an awesome game room on the third floor. What do you like to play?"

"You ask a lot of questions."

She was right. Jake was asking a lot of questions. Not his normal behavior at all. In Jake's rarefied world it wasn't uncommon for women to do the chasing. Then again, it wasn't every day he chatted with a beautiful ti-gress. Jake decided to cut himself some slack and focus on the tender morsel in front of him, the one that if he played his cards right he might get to nibble on before the night was over.

"I get the feeling this might be your first HalloMask party. I'd be more than happy to show you around."

"Thanks, but I'm a big girl who can take care of her-self."

"Then I'll dispense with the pleasantries of how beautiful you are and how I've waited all my life for someone like you to walk into it and go straight to the chase. I'd like nothing more than to peel that costume off of you stripe by stripe and see if the caramel on the inside tastes as sweet as it looks on the outside."

"Oh, so it's like that, huh?"

Her expression was neutral, showing neither desire nor disdain. Yet Jake swore the temperature rose ten degrees. "It's exactly like that."

A second passed. Two. Five.

"Take it easy, Zorro." The woman's mouth curved into a gorgeous smile, revealing sparkling white teeth.

Who was this woman? After a steady diet of drama queens, gold diggers and debutantes, her devil-may-care attitude was as refreshing as rain. Definitely not from the Windy City. Local women didn't emit that type of breeze. Jake wasn't looking for commitment, or even a constant. He was, however, open to a one-night stand, the entire weekend if the lovemaking was good enough. Especially since after this weekend his freedom would be limited, thanks to one of his friends and potential future business partner, Lincoln Trotter. Lincoln, who along with making moves to become one of the wealthiest entrepreneurs in DC was also working as a political consultant for next year's election, had asked Jake to serve as the unofficial local escort for his fiancée, Sasha McDowell. The socialite daughter of the powerfully influential, Washington, DC–based McDowell family, Sasha was coming to Chicago to work with her godmother on a holiday event. Lincoln had entrusted his friend and possible business partner to keep sure-to-come-sniffing Chicagoan alpha wolves at bay. It was a tall order and not the type of responsibility he'd normally shoulder, but Jake had reluctantly agreed. If this was going to be his last totally free weekend until the New Year, a nice, casual sex romp would be the perfect way to spend it. But that was it. Nothing more. No attachments. No strings. Casual dating was his modus

operandi. His best friend and older siblings had all settled into married life. But a trip to the altar wasn't in
his near future. Jake was sure about that.

The tigress turned to leave. Jake didn't want her to
go. Just then, a hit R & B song began to play.

"How about a dance?"

"Maybe later," she threw over her shoulder.

Her graceful retreat gave him an unobstructed view
of her juicy booty, an anatomy strong point. Her tail
swished slowly back and forth. He stood mesmerized,
almost hypnotized, as if a therapist had waved a wand
before his eyes and begun a countdown from ten to one.
He'd been hungry upon arrival and had planned to head
straight for the always bountiful buffet. But a certain
feline had awakened a different kind of appetite, one
he was determined to assuage.

"She's fine, isn't she?"

Jake turned to find Claude, a former PDS resident
and high school classmate, wearing a Rick James styled
wig, dark sunglasses and outlandish rocker garb.

"Damn right. Who is it?"

"That's what almost every man in here has been trying to figure out. So far, no one can place her."

"It's rare to see a stranger here," Jake said, continu-
ing to look in the direction she'd gone even though she'd
become lost in the crowd. "Especially tonight."

Claude nodded, knowing Jake spoke the truth. It was
one of the reasons the partygoers felt comfortable letting their hair down, getting wild and crazy and for
at least twenty-four hours, casting good home train-
ing and social mores to the wind. Those attending felt
safe, knew their reputations were protected. Aside from

the occasional pro athlete, model or A-list celebrity, outsiders weren't normally allowed at the masquerade party. Most of the attendees had known each other since childhood. Trying to keep one's identity from those who knew it best, while sometimes sharing in casual intimacies, was always part of the fun. The attendees, rarely numbering more than a hundred fifty or so, were wealthy, well educated and socially connected, and knew that what happened at the mansion would never be known outside their tight-knit circle. Still, because of the stringent rules regarding who got invited, the men knew she was somebody who knew somebody.

"I see you finally got with protocol." Claude nodded toward Jake's mask.

"A little bit."

Jake adjusted the slightly uncomfortable contraption, one of the reasons that in the past couple years the party had happened, he never bothered putting one on. When arriving at these parties in the past, it was usually straight from work. Tonight, he'd had a couple hours to actually unwind before heading over. His clothing was still business casual sans suit coat, but the simple addition of a black mask had changed how he moved around the room. It had definitely increased his boldness when speaking to the tiger, leading him to believe that maybe the masks were not that bad after all.

"Being mysterious does add to the fun, I guess, though most of us can still guess each other's identities." He looked in the direction of where the temptress had gone. "Except for a certain feline. She's still a stranger."

"If I have my way, she won't be a stranger for long."

Claude's comment rankled. An irrational reaction

but one that couldn't be helped. There was something about the woman that took Jake beyond his usual attraction for beautiful females. There was something about his feelings that felt intimate, almost familiar, even though that made no sense. The thought of her being with someone else was one he didn't want to entertain. Neither did he want to consider the possibility that she might not entertain him either.

"Where's the food?" he asked, for a diversion. "The same setup?"

Claude shook his head. "Grub is on the second floor tonight. The different flow is probably to accommodate the new game on tonight's agenda."

Jake raised a brow. He'd attended this party for the past four years and hadn't bothered to read the invitation past date and time.

"Midnight scavenger hunt."

"That's different. Sounds cool." With his previous ravenousness returning, Jake headed toward the stairs. As he mounted them, a plan began to form. He'd go on a hunt alright, but it would be a specific tigress, not random scavenging, that would be on his mind.

Walking as calmly and naturally as her suddenly noodle-like legs and hammering heart would allow, Sasha made her way through a throng of partygoers. She crossed a smartly appointed living room boasting a twenty-foot Christmas tree, down a hall lined with collectible art and into one of the ostentatious home's fourteen bathrooms. Only then did she release the breath she'd been holding, slumping down on a nearby fur-covered stool. Not at the party ten minutes and already she'd found her target, the man who'd help her implement a daring, slightly lascivious and completely uncharacteristic plan she'd cooked up only days before. Sasha wanted to experience what it was like to be free. Incognito. How it felt to move in a place where no one knew her name, or her family. No one knew her dad. No one knew the weight that rested on the shoulder of any child bearing the McDowell name. Having secretly broken an engagement the month before leaving DC, Sasha also wanted to live out a fantasy, to experience a no holds barred, no strings attached sexual encounter with a man whom she was drawn to on physical energy alone.

That was not the type of intimacy she'd had since dating Lincoln. Sex with him had been average, predictable, with her almost always left wanting. Lincoln's bedroom antics were as conservative as his political beliefs. The one time she'd suggested oral sex, he'd been so aghast one would have thought she'd asked permission to bite off his penis. Doggy style was about as naughty as he'd get. What would it be like to feel the way those women in the Harlequin Blaze novels she and her friends used to read at school felt? To be sexed into orgasm, left shivering and weak, delirious with pleasure? Did that really only happen in books and movies?

Sasha wanted to know, and she felt that a party like the one she was now attending may be one of the only ways she could ever safely find out. Reign, a sister of Lincoln's good friend, Jake Eddington, had told her about HalloMask during a recent phone call. She'd laughed conspiratorially as she'd shared some of the shenanigans that went on there. As soon as the call ended, Sasha devised a plan and set it in motion. She worked quickly, before rationality took over and she changed her mind. The plan worked. Now here she was, with weak knees and a wet vagina, fantasizing about how to get Zorro into bed.

There was only one potential land mine she had to watch out for—Jake, the man who would undoubtedly be Lincoln's eyes and ears for the duration of her Point du Sable stay. Not that she didn't want to see him. To the contrary, if she had her truest wish come true, her sexual escapade would be with Reign's brother. But to count off the reasons he was off-limits would take all her fingers and toes. Still, from the time her godmother invited her to Chicago, she'd thought about getting closer with Jake—a difficult task given his relationship with Lincoln, one made nearly impossible after learning the very man she secretly desired romantically had been made *her* protector, by her ex-fiancé no less, charged with keeping away any would-be suitors. That they'd secretly broken up didn't matter. Sasha knew why Lincoln had taken the news so calmly. It was because he thought that this time would be like the others. That a month would go by, maybe two, and she'd change her mind. He was wrong. She wouldn't. As soon as the holidays were over, she'd make the announcement. Then her ex would know for sure.

Her desires for Jake didn't matter, especially tonight. According to Reign, there was only a slim chance he'd even be there. The party was happening on the same night as a Bears football game, a team boasting several of Jake's clients and against a rival team that he almost never missed. "If he does show up," Reign had told her, "he won't be wearing a mask."

"Why not?"

"Probably because my cocky brother doesn't want to cover his thinks-he's-handsome-but-not-really face. He usually dresses up as himself."

Upon arrival, Sasha had taken a quick turn around all three floors. There were several men there not wearing masks. Jake had not been among them. His absence, at least for now, had been a huge relief and gave her the freedom she needed to truly be this new, adventurous version of herself. It was how she'd been able to walk up to a stranger and shamelessly flirt without the fear of someone watching and reporting her to Lincoln. Or her brothers. Or her parents.

Shaking away thoughts of exes and family and DC, Sasha refocused on the task at hand. *You've met him, your boy toy for the evening. Now what?*

Good question. For the first time since putting this cockamamie plan into action, Sasha allowed herself the luxury of actually thinking about what she was doing, to question the wisdom of carrying out the ballsy plan for the secret seduction of a total stranger, of taking advantage of an opportunity that might not ever come again.

The idea had sounded good at the time. In her mind. Back in the comfy confines of her suburban DC bedroom. Just after ending the call with Jake's sister Reign. She'd called to say she wouldn't be there to welcome Sasha when she arrived Sunday morning, that a last-minute model cancellation had her flying out to the West Coast to bail out a clothing designer friend. While chatting, Reign casually mentioned something else she'd be missing, the HalloMask affair, one of the Chicago elite's must-attend parties of the year. Elaborate costumes were key, she'd explained, designed to hide one's identity from a room of people who knew each other best. That was part of the night's challenge, to see who could stay totally incognito the longest, although Reign had admitted that before the night was over many identities were guessed correctly.

It was a super private affair. But getting the details was easy. Reign had been more than happy to tell the suddenly super-interested Sasha all about the swanky mansion, the detailed invitation and the four-digit code that only invitees knew. She was a dear family friend who wasn't even going to be in town until Sunday. What could it hurt? A plan began hatching almost immediately. One that would allow her to do something bold and uncharacteristic, to shed the very public, controlled persona that as the daughter of an ambassador, a prominent insider on Capitol Hill, she was perpetually chained to. As far back as she could remember, Sasha's every move had been monitored, her life carefully planned. Her wardrobe, schooling, even love life was scrutinized and rid of any potential scandal. Even her fiancé had been parent-encouraged and approved, which was why a month after ending the relationship, the breakup was still tightly under wraps. Her now ex had asked her to keep this new development a secret. "Until you return from Chicago," he'd added, undoubtedly thinking she'd change her mind, as had happened the other times she'd tried to end something that had never truly worked for her. This time was different. She was different. Yet she agreed to wait to break the news, partly because he'd asked but mostly because she wasn't looking forward to ruining everyone's holiday season, or the family fallout her decision would cause.

Less than an hour after hanging up with Reign, Sasha had changed her flight plans, hired a car service and booked a room at one of Chicago's upscale hotels. She then phoned her godmother and let her know that she wouldn't need picking up at the airport, but would join her for the scheduled brunch at the Eddington estate. Her fiancé, Lincoln, hadn't questioned the change in plans. Her parents didn't know about them. They loved and trusted Lincoln and would assume the night before flying to Chicago she was with him. They'd never think to guess otherwise. To them, she was still the shy, sheltered boarding school student who obeyed all the rules, not the confident, daring woman of twenty-four who'd once sneaked a boyfriend into her all-girls Swiss prep school or who, on a dare, had traveled across Europe alone.

The plan had been implemented perfectly. She'd arrived in town, gotten checked in and changed at the hotel and been driven over to the swanky neighborhood where the party was held. Only a tad of apprehension had entered as she placed fingers on the keypad and tapped in the code. When the door opened to a crowd of people, the sounds of music and laughter and the smell of amazing food, socialite Sasha felt at home. She'd gotten familiar with her surroundings and then spotted Zorro, everything a girl could want in a fantasy, and a whole host of butterflies had begun swarming again. She'd known immediately. He was the one. No way a man who could make her melt within seconds and without touching would not be frickin' awesome in bed.

There was only one thing more frightening than putting together a ridiculous scheme. Going through with it.

Someone jiggled the door handle, rousing Sasha from her thoughts. "Just a sec!"

Sasha rose from the stool, wet one of the rolled towels with cold water and gently cooled her flushed face. She pulled lipstick and a powder compact from the furry clutch she'd purchased to match her outfit. After freshening her makeup and fluffing the waist-length golden wig, she took a deep breath and opened the door. A completely masked Black Panther was there to greet her.

"Sorry," she mumbled, as she stepped right to pass him.

Panther cut her off. "Whoa, slow down there, you sexy kitten. What say we get to know one another, you know, cat to cat."

She placed her arms in the superhero's popular pose. "*Wakanda Forever*!" she replied, before backing away.

"Hey, wait!"

Sasha hurried down the hall and up a flight of stairs, where what looked to be a fully-stocked professional bar was positioned at the far end of the room. There were fewer people up here and no sign of Zorro. Taking a deep breath, she slowed her pace and crossed over to get a glass of wine from the friendly bartender, then sat in a chair nearby. The accent chair was partially hidden by another of the home's large Christmas trees, a perfect vantage point from which to check out the crowd and plot her next move. For the next thirty minutes, Sasha enjoyed playing the voyeur—sipping a second glass of good vintage vino and downing a small plate of scrumptious finger food. Reign had been right about the costumes, as clandestine as they were outlandish. Lots of wigs, sunglasses and full-faced masks boasting superheroes, celebrity look-alikes and movie characters; most identities were indeed hidden. Since he was wearing all black paired with a simple mask, Zorro's costume had been one of the more revealing.

She'd hardly finished thinking of him when her tempting target appeared at the top of the stairs. He wasn't alone. Cardi B was beside him. Or perhaps it was a long-haired Rihanna. Whichever star the woman's costume was meant to copy, she looked beautiful in her skintight sequined gown, oversize shades, long black wig and five-inch Louboutins. She hung on to his arm and from the looks of things, his every word. Sasha felt an unwarranted stab of jealousy and was relieved when the woman laughed at something Jake said, squeezing his arm before walking over to a food-laden table. Sasha knew it was time to make her move, let him know she was interested before someone else staked a claim. In his costume, he might be mistaken for Zorro, or the Lone Ranger. But if this party was anything like some that she'd been to, he wouldn't be alone for long.

Two

A slight frown marred Jake's handsome face. He'd been looking-not-looking for almost an hour and in this instant could have sworn that he actually smelled the distinct perfume of the stranger that with a smile and less than one hundred words had captured his interest completely. Just before deciding to give up, he looked up to see the object of tonight's desire heading his way. She was looking at her cell phone, texting away, while maneuvering between the guests dotting the space between them and heading toward the stairs. He couldn't let her get away.

"There you are," he said, staying her progress with a soft hand and managing a cool tone even though his heartbeat increased.

She looked up. "Oh, hey."

"Enjoying the party?"

"It's okay."

Her comment elicited a slightly raised brow. There were people who'd been trying to crash the HalloMask party for years.

"Just okay? You're not enjoying yourself?"

Sasha smiled, a move that brightened the room and made the cute little whiskers on her half mask bob this way and that. She had balanced features, smooth skin and what in the brighter upstairs light looked to be a hint of a dimple twinkling from beneath the bottom of her furry cat mask.

"I've been to better parties. But this mansion," Sasha paused and looked around, "is one of the most impressive I've seen. The food is delicious. I guess all I need to increase the rating of this holiday gathering is to take you up on that dance you offered."

A smile split Jake's face. "Now we're talking. Let's go."

He placed a hand on her arm, then felt a nudge on his. "Take this."

Elaine. Just that quickly, Sasha had wiped out Jake's memory of not coming upstairs alone.

Elaine held out a small saucer filled with delicacies. "I know you said you weren't hungry, but these truffle mac-n-cheese bites are delicious. You've got to try them. And the wrapped mini dogs with bourbon BBQ sauce dip? Yum!"

"Sorry," Jake whispered, as he eased his hand from Sasha's arm and reached for the saucer that Elaine presented. Only then did his longtime friend with occasional benefits seem to realize that something had been interrupted.

"Excuse me, honey," Elaine said, swinging her waist-length wig and adopting a caricature-like Spanish accent. "But this is my man!"

Jake was thankful that lady tiger managed a smile.

"Ah, so you're Cardi B. I wondered whether the costume was her or Rihanna."

"Well, now you know, Okurrr?"

The melodious sound of laughter poured out of the cat's mouth. Jake laughed too. Elaine's imitation of the famous rapper was spot-on.

She smiled at Elaine and winked at Jake. "Have fun."

Before Jake could respond or stop her, she turned and headed upstairs to the third floor.

"Damn, Elaine," he said, clearly irritated. "Why'd you do that?"

"Just playing the role." She lifted Jackie O style sunglasses and gazed at Jake. "You're not mad at me, are you?"

For the second time tonight, Jake was actually more peeved than he cared to admit but didn't let it show. He lightly shook his head, popped a mac-n-cheese ball into his mouth and after downing the tasty bite said, "Naw, it's all good."

"Who is that anyway?"

"The cat?" He shrugged. "I dunno."

"Rare that someone remains a mystery to me, mask or no. But she doesn't look familiar."

"You know the organizers like to shake it up now and then by inviting a celebrity or whatnot."

Elaine stared in the direction Sasha had gone. "You think she's famous?"

"Could be." Jake finished the finger food and set the plate on a table nearby. "You're right. That food's really good. Thanks for bringing it over. Think I'll head over to the bar for a drink to wash it down."

"I'll go with you."

Damn. Losing Elaine was going to be harder to shake than Jake realized.

He ordered a beer. Elaine chose a dirty martini. After a couple sips, she said, "What do you say we go somewhere private where I can finish my food, we can finish our drinks and then, you know," she wriggled her brows, "maybe have a party of our own."

"Sounds tempting," Jake managed while not being tempted at all. "But tonight, I'm going to be good."

"I have no doubt about that, which is why I want you all to myself."

Jake leaned forward and gave Elaine a chaste kiss on the cheek. "Not tonight, love. Thanks for the refreshments, though. If you'll excuse me, I think I'll go mix and mingle."

While mentally he was being drawn to the third floor and the direction of the tigress, Jake casually sauntered downstairs and took a turn around the home's massive rooms. There he ran into superheroes, movie and TV characters, A-list celebrities, even a slick-haired, gold-lamé suit-wearing brother nailing a serious dance impression of a 60s' James Brown. He spoke to a few friends he recognized, and after patiently listening to a pitch from an up-and-coming boxer looking for an agent, even after explaining he wasn't one, eased back up the stairs to the third floor and hoped he hadn't missed her.

It was quieter there, with dimmed, recessed lighting further adding to the tranquil atmosphere. There was a large circular landing. He looked around and noted several closed doors, and the glow of a night-light coming from a bathroom door, which was open. He headed in that direction. At the end of that hall was the game room and the murmur of conversation. Cat woman perhaps? His heart quickened. A quick peek inside dashed his hopes. There were several people chatting it up. A few guests played throwback arcade games while others flirted on bar stools and watched a lively game of shuffleboard. Jake stepped out of the room and headed back in the direction he'd come. He was almost to the landing area when a door opened and a soft *psst* sounded in his ear. He turned toward an entrance opened only wide enough to allow the tail of a tiger costume to be swished quickly back and forth before being pulled back inside the darkened space. That small sign was all the encouragement Jake needed. With a quick look around, he placed a hand on the knob, turned it and stepped inside.

He smelled her. That unrecognizable scent that had teased him all evening tickled his nose once again.

"What perfume is that?"

She chuckled. "That's what you want to do? Talk about cologne?"

"I want to see you."

"No!" And then softer. "No lights. Keep on your mask. Take off your clothes."

"What?" The command was wanted, but unexpected.

"Unless you want to have sex fully clothed."

Her directness was like a shot of adrenaline to Jake's loins. Blood surged to his penis, engorging the head. After locking the door, he undid his belt buckle, letting the sound of unzipping metal be his answer to her demand. Hearing the sound of rustling fabric had him imagining his personal pussycat easing onto the bed. His actions quickened. With only a sliver of moon coming through a partially opened blind to guide him, he reached the bed. Slipping off his sporty Gambini loafers, he felt a set of fingernails slide across his back. He stood, removed a condom from his wallet, then repocketed his wallet into his slacks before removing them and his boxers in one fell swoop.

By now another scent had joined the spicy, floral fragrance worn by his temptress. The smell of her. A moan confirmed that she'd jumped ahead of him in the pleasure game, had literally taken matters into her own hands. The thought was hella sexy and changed his plans to get completely naked. Instead, he rolled over and collided with a soft, bare thigh. A hand slid down the side of his face, damp with his lover's juices. The smell was sweet, intoxicating, with hints of vanilla and cinnamon as from a gooey roll. He kissed her thigh. Licked the bared flesh. Ran a hand up her body and realized the mini had been pulled up to her waist. She still wore the thigh-high stilettos, and the mask.

Damn!

She shifted until his face was positioned over her paradise. Gyrating hips clearly told him what she wanted next. Who was he to argue or make her wait? He kissed her there, through a lacy thong. She placed a hand on the back of his head, encouraging a deeper exchange.

He obliged, used a finger to move aside the lace and his tongue to slide down her wet pussy's slit. She tasted like ambrosia. The room felt like heaven. If he didn't know any better, he would have sworn music played. Instead, it was the whispered mewling of a satisfied partner, mumbling her bliss as he French kissed her nether lips and teased her pearl.

"So good." She continued to grind—slowly, rhythmically—against his mouth. "So good. So good. Ah, ah!"

His performance was good. Jake knew that. He wasn't cocky, but among the fairer sex his oral skills were legendary. More than one woman had sworn his tongue held magical power. Others had warned that it was a lethal weapon that should be registered with the state.

He parted her lips with his fingers, slipping one long digit into the depths of her heat. Her hips rose from the bed. Her legs began to tremble. He continued to lick, suck, bite, kiss, until she lost all control. He felt her thrashing, heard the light scream that a pillow had muffled. His dick, already pulsating, was now rock-hard. He slid on the condom, watched as his siren got on all fours and presented her ass for his pleasure. He reverently grasped each meaty globe, massaging them as he ran his sex up and down her crease.

His mind whirled with a singular question. Who was this goddess? The sex hadn't even been completed before knowing he wanted her again. He leaned down to kiss the dimples winking at him from the soft glow of the moon. Only then did he notice a dragonfly tattoo. A quick turn of his mental Rolodex yielded nothing. Jake was an observant man. He was into tats and would remember one as colorful and unusual as the one he now licked. With his body throbbing, there was no more time to try and fit puzzle pieces. The only thing he wanted to connect was his stem to her flower. After positioning himself at her opening, he did just that in one long, deep thrust.

She felt incredible. Every nerve ending spazzed at the feel of her tightness. She shimmied back against him, setting him all the way off. He placed a hand on each hip, closed his eyes and experienced ecstasy. In, out, pumping, pushing, they connected over and again. He eased her body onto the bed, lying in a way their whole bodies touched. He kissed her, and almost exploded. Her lips. So soft. Her tongue. So tentatively teasing. Her body. So perfectly aligned with his. He lifted her leg and reentered a spot he'd already claimed as his own. She gave as good as she got, wriggling her hips to take him in deeper, running her nails across the small of his back. They settled into a slow rhythm as though this wasn't the first time the two had made love. He could have gone on for an hour, or a day. But his groin was ready to burst. She could feel it too. She wrapped her legs around him, welcoming his vigorous thrusts. She hissed, digging her nails into his back as her second orgasm collided with his first. Afterward, they lay on their backs and caught their breath. Jake wasn't typically a cuddler, but tonight he reached over to pull the woman whose name he still did not know into his arms. She refused, instead rising from the bed.

"I'm going to take a quick shower," she told him. "When I come out, please be gone."

He rolled to his side, feeling dejected. "What's your name?"

"Better we maintain the mystery."

Jake didn't see that being better at all.

"You were incredible," she offered, just before entering the en suite. "Take care of yourself, Zorro."

She closed the door. He heard the lock click behind her and the shower engaged. Jake fell back against the bed, utterly confused and totally spent. On top of his already full schedule, another assignment just got dumped on his plate. Uncover the identity of this sexy cat lady. No matter how hard he had to work for it or how long it took, Jake vowed to make this brainteaser one that he solved.

Three

The invigorating intro to a current pop hit awoke Sasha from a deep, peaceful sleep. Eyes closed, she reached over and groped for her phone, then opened one eye to tap off the alarm. She stretched and shifted positions. Her eyes flew open. She sat up straight. A delicate ache between her legs reminded her of last night's shenanigans. She'd done it! She'd pulled off her crazy scheme and actually made love to a fantasy man. A complete stranger. She'd gone and had herself a one-night stand and darn it if she didn't feel right amazing about it. Being with Zorro was everything and more than she thought it would be but still…what the heck had she been thinking!

Grabbing a pillow and clutching it to her chest, she eased back onto the mattress and relived each luscious second of the delectable exchange. Zorro's body, toned and powerful. His lips, soft and tasty. His tongue, skilled and purposeful. His dick, commanding and… Sasha threw back the covers and hopped out of bed. Now was not the time to remember…all of that. Not when she'd be seeing her godmother in just over an hour, and presumably her unofficial guardian, Jake, his parents Derrick and Mona, and the entire Eddington family shortly after that. Not when she'd have to lock away the femme fatale persona from last night and pull out the demure, quiet daughter of a politician that the town of Point was expecting. Sasha didn't fancy herself an actress. Last night's role aside, she hadn't played a character since middle school's Cinderella production. But today, to keep her secret, she'd have to pull off an award-winning performance. To have experienced a life-changing sexual encounter yet act as though she were the same person as before the memorable tryst would be quite the feat.

Hours later, and her body almost still tingled. Rubbing her hands together, she imagined the weight of her lover's tight butt, could feel his fingertips skimming across her bare skin. If the idea wasn't simply batshit bonkers, she'd even fancy herself a little in love. The intimacy had been just that good. Could she do it? Could she walk into a room of people who knew her and hide the experience she felt etched across her face? Sasha quelled the oncoming panic. It was either pull it off or cause the one thing her family abhorred—scandal. That, Sasha knew, was not going to happen. Neither was it possible to undo what had occurred last night. Best to pull out her manners and put on her poise. Time to prepare for the show.

By the time Sasha checked out of the hotel and spoke to the driver she'd hired, last night's emboldened tigress had been tamed. The wig was gone, the entire costume in fact now at the bottom of one of the hotel's dumpsters. In its place was a navy designer pantsuit with matching four-inch pumps and a three-strand pearl necklace. A wool cape coat from an upcoming DC designer was sprawled across the backseat. Her thick shoulder-length hair had been flat-ironed to perfection in the hotel's salon and given a slight flip at the ends. A fringed bang further softened the look and helped emphasize one of Sasha's best features, her doe-like brown eyes. The heavy MAC makeup worn last night to further conceal her identity had been replaced with a scant dusting of powder, light mascara and clear gloss. Instead of the twenty-four years she currently boasted, she could have easily passed for a teen.

Except for a text from her ex-boyfriend Lincoln, one she ignored, the short drive from Chicago to the township of Point du Sable was uneventful. Sasha tried not to think about him and the problems awaiting back home as she admired the architecture and well-maintained landscapes while passing through the town's center. She'd been honest with Lincoln and glad she'd ended their relationship. Still, a shard of guilt rode along with her in the limo, as did the imagined imprint of Zorro's hand on her flesh. If keeping such illicit thoughts proved as difficult later as they did right now, she was in for a doozy of an afternoon.

After a right here, a left there and a couple more

turns, they entered a neighborhood of medium-sized houses with expansive front lawns. Her godmother's home was at the center of a cul-de-sac, outstanding and grandiose, just like the woman waving from the home's arched, double front doors.

"Val!"

"Sasha!"

The two women hugged each other enthusiastically, shared air kisses then embraced again.

"My, aren't you a sight for these tired, old eyes."

"Get out of here with that. You don't look tired, and you are not old."

Val tsked and said, "Amazing what an expertly applied layer of makeup can do."

She paused as the driver delivered the last of Sasha's luggage, then reached for the nearest handle and tugged the rolling case. Sasha grabbed the grips of the remaining two and followed her inside. They continued through the foyer and down a long narrow hallway to a large, airy guest room boasting various shades of green.

"Why did you hire a car, darlin'? I would have been more than happy to pick you up from your flight."

"Oh no worries, Val, really. It happened due to a last-minute change in plans." Sasha told her about Reign's unexpected trip to California, and how because of it she'd miss this week's brunch. Not the real reason why Sasha hired a car but not a complete lie either.

"Either way, I'm very glad you're here." Val walked over and opened the door to a walk-in closet. "Here's where you can hang your things. And that dresser is empty. Make yourself at home."

"Thanks, Val. I'll unpack later."

"Good idea." She led them out of the room and back down the hall to the living area. "Valencia sends her love and thanks you for helping out in her absence. She said she'd call you sometime next week."

"How is your daughter? Still saving the world?"

"Absolutely. She signed up for another stint, even though I tried to talk her out of it. While incredibly proud of her contribution to Doctors Without Borders, I miss her terribly, and reminded her that she'd promised to help me this year."

"Clearly, she didn't go with you on that guilt trip."

"Nope, the only trip she took was from Malaysia to Ethiopia, her new location for the next six months. She wants me to visit this spring."

"You totally should."

"You've been there?"

"No, but every country in Africa I've seen has its own unique brand of beauty."

"I'm thinking about it. For now, however, it's time to focus on your stay and the upcoming holidays. An Eddington brunch is the perfect way to kick it off!" Val crossed over to a hall closet and retrieved a faux fur coat. "Do you need to freshen up, dear, or can we get going? I'm starved."

"Me too. I'm all set and ready to attend one of these famous gatherings I've heard so much about."

"Mona is the hostess with the mostest. You're in for a treat."

Of that, Sasha had no doubt. But not for the reasons Val probably imagined. All night long, her time with the hot stranger had replayed in her mind. But today she'd see another temptation, one whose identity she did know. She'd always secretly admired her brother TJ's and Lincoln's friend from a distance—through his internet and social media presence. Her feelings on seeing Jake, whom she'd only met in passing a time or two, were an even mix of anticipation and dread. Fluttery feelings at the thought of seeing him again after so many years. Dread at the possibility of being even more attracted to Jake than she'd been to Zorro, only this time not being able to do a damn thing about it.

Last night's party mansion was mammoth, but upon entering the property known as Eddington Estate, Sasha determined it was no less impressive. As they neared the main house at the top of the hill, a sense of excitement bubbled in Sasha's gut. Anxiety showed up, too, but Sasha did her best to ignore that pesky feeling. With her godmother's constant chatter and the picturesque surroundings, Sasha could almost forget she was about to be in the same room with a man easily as sexy as last night's sin.

Val pulled around to the back of the home, which featured a solarium made of almost all glass. Sasha loved nature and immediately decided this was one of the home's best details. The goings-on inside were obscured by tall leafy plants but she noticed a stream that flowed from the inside out, with koi casually swimming inside the covered, heated structure. Sasha was not unaccustomed to wealth but before stepping a toe across the Eddington threshold, it was clear that she was in rarified air.

"My gracious but that is one handsome man."

Sasha looked over as a tall guy who could only be described as beautiful unfolded himself from a snazzy two-toned Bugatti and strode toward the passenger side of the car.

"Who is that?"

Before Val could answer, the gentleman had reached the area between them and nodded a greeting as he opened the passenger door. A woman, as stunning as the man was handsome, eased out of the sporty low-riding vehicle and beamed a smile at Val. It was a face that Sasha immediately recognized—Jake's older sister Maeve. From the wedding photos splashed across TV and social media, Sasha knew the man accompanying Maeve must be her husband, an attorney, Victor Cortez.

The couple turned to the comparatively modest Cadillac sedan transporting Val and Sasha. Victor opened Val's door. Val stepped out. As Maeve leaned in to hug Val, Sasha exited the vehicle and walked around to meet them.

"Mrs. Baldwin, you look lovely. A pleasure to see you again." Maeve turned to the man beside her. "You've met Victor, my husband."

"Of course," Val replied. The two spoke and shook hands. "This is Sasha McDowell," she continued, after the introductions. "In Valencia's absence, she's generously agreed to help with this year's holiday drive."

"Your group always does such a great job providing clothing, food, toys and other necessities during this season. I can't wait to hear more. Let's go inside."

Sasha took a calming breath. They entered a room, stunning in its seamless mix of the indoors with the outdoors, highlighted by koi-filled streams and shrilling birds perched in the trees. There were more than a dozen people milling about, and gloved waiters hoisting trays of what looked like mimosas and some kind of finger food wrapped in pastry dough. Sasha thought the jazzy music playing was being piped in through hidden speakers until she looked over and spotted a one-man band behind an electronic keyboard. His skills were impressive. It sounded like several musicians playing.

An older woman broke away from a group and came over to greet them. Sasha didn't remember what Mona looked like but knew it was her before Val spoke the name when they hugged, and Maeve made proper reintroductions. That she was the queen of this castle shone through in her carriage, and the ease with which she quietly commanded the room. Sasha met two other ladies, sisters-in-love as Mona described them, and with the help of a delicious mimosa had just begun to relax when Jake entered the room.

Their eyes met. The room crackled with their energy's electricity. Sasha was surprised at how strongly her body reacted. He looked easygoing and felt…comfortable. His appearance was even more appetizing than the aromas she smelled. More attractive in person than on social media or TV. An ivory sweater complemented his bronzed skin. A pair of tan slacks showed off a pair of legs that emphasized power and cupped a tight butt that immediately produced a memory of the one she'd squeezed last night. A pair of Timberlands took the look from preppy to cool, giving him a sexy street swag even better than his wealth could produce. His face looked freshly shaven. A tiny diamond stud twinkled from his left ear. She processed all of this in the seconds it took him to cross the room and greet his mom with a kiss.

"Jake, darling, you remember Ambassador McDowell's daughter, Sasha McDowell."

"I remember a Sasha," he said, reaching out slowly to take her hand in his. "A kid with braces and ponytails. But I don't remember this exquisite young lady." He brushed his lips across her knuckles.

"It's a pleasure to see you again," Sasha managed around the clump of nerves restricting her airway.

"Trust me, the pleasure's all mine."

Mona cleared her throat. "I understand congratulations are in order," she said pointedly, her voice silky smooth even as narrowed eyes shifted in Jake's direction.

Under Jake's spell, Sasha drew a blank. "Ma'am?"

"Your engagement? To be…married?"

"Oh, yes, that." Sasha pressed a hand against her upper chest and tried to regain a control that was obviously slipping. She pasted on what she hoped to be a believable smile. The questionable way Val looked at her proved her act was only partially convincing.

"Thank you."

"When's the wedding?" Val asked.

"We, um, haven't set a date."

"How is TJ, Sasha?" Jake asked. "We've exchanged texts here and there but other than a brief conversation last week, haven't talked in a while."

She could have kissed him, and not just because of the subject change. "Being an annoying big brother, as usual."

Her answer broke the tension as she hoped it might.

"He called me last week," Jake continued. "As did your fiancé. But you know about that, though."

Sasha barely managed to not roll an eye. "Yes, he told me."

"Told you what, exactly?"

"Right now," Mona interrupted, "that answer will have to wait. I need to get this brunch officially started. Sasha, Val, you two are seated at my table."

Mona briefly greeted the guests and once seated, introduced Sasha around the table. Theirs was a table of women who along with Val and Mona included Avery, the sister-in-love she'd met earlier, Avery's mother-in-love, Tami, and Willow, a woman who assisted Avery with a booming event planning business. Conversation flowed as freely as the mimosas. Sasha appreciated that it mostly went on without her. She busied herself downing a silky butternut squash soup first course followed by an arugula salad. She was sure her entrée choice of Cajun snapper over "dirty" rice with roasted asparagus was as delicious as the other courses. Too bad, because Sasha didn't taste a thing. Her appetite had been highjacked, her mind preoccupied with the man sitting at a table within her peripheral vision, one whose eyes she swore she could feel on her. For one wild moment it wasn't Jake but Zorro eyeing her, remembering, as she did, what happened last night. Except that wasn't possible. Jake wasn't at the party. He didn't know about her adventure with the super sexy stranger, or that her body had been played as fluidly last night as today's musician tickled his keyboard. It was all Sasha could do not to turn and stare outright, or better yet, throw all caution to the wind, come clean with Jake about her attraction and continue her newfound sexual freedom. By the time the dessert tray was rolled around, she forced her mind back into the present, determined to properly display the boarding school social skills that had cost her parents a mint.

It wasn't too difficult. She and Willow, who worked with Avery at On Point, were around the same age and had a lot in common, including both spending time in Switzerland and speaking fluent French. They conversed in that language a bit while making their final course choices. Her appetite finally back, Sasha chose a caramel pecan bar topped with homemade vanilla ice cream and hot dark chocolate. She took one bite and was transported back to the Alps as the gooey caramel, the crunchy nuts, the creamy ice and the hot dark chocolate all came together in a perfect symphony.

"How is it?" Willow asked around her bite of deep-dish apple pie topped with the same vanilla ice cream.

"So good," Sasha responded, while reaching for another bite. "So, so good!"

Kind of like her night with Zorro, she thought, her noni muscles clenching at the mere memory of that hot caramel experience. The decadent dessert she now enjoyed was almost as good, but not quite.

Four

"Um, that is...*so good*!"

Jake was walking behind Sasha's chair but within earshot when she said the words seared in his memory from last night's rendezvous. He almost tripped over his Tims but managed to keep walking. Hard to do when one's head was about to explode.

Sasha was the tigress? TJ's sister, Lincoln's fiancée, was the one from last night who'd taken her tight body and turned him out? No effing way.

He bypassed the very visible bar where he'd been heading and continued on to the restroom and tried to reconcile his impossible thoughts. He spent extra time washing his hands and replaying last night's love fest in his mind. He tried to recall the facial features the mask left uncovered, along with every other physical attribute of the stranger he could bring to mind. He looked at his own face with its deer-in-headlights expression and sighed audibly. Last night's dream couldn't turn into today's nightmare. Sasha couldn't be the tiger. That would mess up everything.

He reentered the main room determined to find out if the impossible was correct. Fortunately, with service over, many had gotten up to chat with guests at other tables. Sasha was standing near where she'd eaten, talking with Avery and her husband, Cayden—Jake's best friend. The setup was perfect. He pushed through a set of nerves and entered their space.

He gave a nod to Cayden and said, "I see you've met Sasha."

"I have. Avery's impressed and," he turned his attention to Sasha, "my wife doesn't impress easily."

He continued speaking with Jake. "Avery's angling to do her wedding, then after the honeymoon have them relocate here and join On Point."

"Wow, her whole life rearranged in a single afternoon." Jake's expression was one of mock admiration as he looked at Avery, covering the sick feeling brought on by the thought of Sasha being last night's mystery kitten but married and unavailable for an entire lifetime. "I think that's a record, girl."

Avery nudged Jake and swatted at Cayden. "Pay these two troublemakers no mind. My work and resume speak for themselves. It's why Val has twice hired me to do her event. I know DC has its own social landscape and I'm sure there are wedding planners worth their weight in gold. But On Point has a special way of capturing the essence of whomever we work with and adding unique touches that make ours the most memorable events around. As I said, check out the reviews on our website, along with the photos from some of the weddings we've done. I'm very proud of the work we've put out there and would hold it up next to anyone."

"Alright, honey, that's enough work for one Sunday," Cayden gently chided. "Did you get a chance to say hello to Bob?"

Avery looked over to where Tami and her friend Bob were talking with Mona and Derrick, Jake's dad. "No, and I haven't spoken to Derrick either." She turned to Sasha. "I'm looking forward to our lunch date next week. I'm sure Willow is too. And I promise the talk won't be all about work."

Jake and Sasha watched as Cayden playfully dragged Avery away. An awkward silence followed their quiet laughter and Jake's attention shifted from the couple to Sasha. His eyes did a slow travel from head to toe and back. She looked shorter than the pussycat he'd pleasured last night but that could be a simple difference in heel size. He studied her pretty, heart-shaped face, almond-shaped eyes and lips he could imagine that he'd kissed before.

"Why are you staring?"

"Oh, was I staring?" Jake asked, still scrutinizing.

"Yes, you're staring. It's borderline rude." He continued looking at her, studying her. Sasha shifted from one leg to the other.

"When is Reign getting back in town?"

Jake crossed his arms and began his interrogation. "When did you get here?"

"What?"

"You heard me. When did you arrive in Chicago?"

"This morning. Why?"

"Because I want to know." What he did next could only be categorized as temporary insanity. He stepped toward her and sniffed.

Yep, her eyes told him he'd lost it. Kudos to her, though. She played it off. Meanwhile he was beginning to think that maybe, just maybe, his suspicions were simply that.

When she spoke, her voice was low and measured. "You're weird."

The tigress's cologne had been unmistakable. Sasha didn't smell like that. Still, something about something he couldn't put his finger on wouldn't let him leave the subject. Not quite yet.

"Did you attend a party last night?"

Her hesitation in responding was so slight it was as though he imagined it. "A party?"

"Yeah, you know, one of those things where a bunch of people get together and music is played. There's usually food and—"

"Jake, I know the definition of a party."

"Were you there last night, wearing a reddish-blond, curly wig and dressed like a tiger?"

He thought her laughter overly bright but then again, he might have been imagining discomfort where there was none.

"Well, were you?"

"I know Lincoln and TJ asked you to look out for me. I appreciate it, but seriously, you inquiring of my every move is not only unnecessary but I can see that it could quickly become downright irritating."

"Does that mean you don't want to tell me where you were last night?"

"I was preparing to come here, to Point du Sable, to help my godmother, Val Baldwin, put on her annual holiday drive. Want to see my plane ticket?"

He raised a brow. "Do you have it on you?"

Sasha's expression made him laugh out loud.

She looked beyond him and waved. "Bye, Jake."

He turned in time to see Val walking over with one of the women Jake remembered being a regular at the PDS Country Club. He wanted to keep questioning Sasha. He wanted to keep doing anything that kept her around. She may not be the party pussycat, but she was equally captivating. Engaged, or not.

But she is engaged. Which means unavailable. TJ's your boy with lots of connections. Lincoln could very well become your partner in the DC business venture you've planned. Don't defecate where you dine.

These were the thoughts that followed him once he left home and headed over to the country club for a game of basketball with friends. Jake wasn't one for following rules but he'd never knowingly try and break up a relationship either. Sasha said she hadn't attended the HalloMask party. That should have made him happy. Somehow it didn't. By the time he'd reached the club and headed into the gym, he'd had a major attitude adjustment. Sasha not having attended the party meant that the beautiful woman with whom he'd had amazing sex with was still out there. Somewhere. Jake was not only a patient man, but a determined one. Then and there, he set a goal. Find the tigress. He wouldn't stop until he did.

Five

Sasha was thankful for the busy week. She'd had a pleasant conversation with Val's daughter Valencia. She'd joined Val at the committee meeting for the food, clothing and toy drive and been given the responsibility of reaching out to potential sponsors outside Chicago. Along with her own contacts, Val had provided a list to cold call, not Sasha's strongest suit but a definite way to help keep her mind off Zorro. And Jake.

Jake had been at the HalloMask party. He'd described her costume to a tee. But how could that be when Reign said he wouldn't be there and if so, he wouldn't be wearing a mask. Zorro wore a mask. At one point, that's almost all he'd had on.

Jake. Zorro. Images of both men flashed through her mind. Very different yet in some ways strikingly similar at the same time. Their height, for instance, and skin tone. That smile. Those lips. Since seeing him at the brunch and being questioned about the party, an incredible scenario began to form in her mind. An impossible possibility. An inconceivable coincidence.

Jake Eddington was Zorro. Zorro was Jake Eddington. Her secret lover was her ex-fiancé's business colleague and potential associate in an international consulting business partnership.

No. That couldn't be true. No way could they be one and the same. Was there? She pulled up images of Jake on social media. Studied the lower half of his face. His stance, and overall demeanor. Over time she could no longer deny it. What had possibly happened was even worse than what her ex-fiancé feared. The one tasked with basically chaperoning her around town may also be her secret lover. Zorro could be Jake. Jake could be Zorro. The sex that night had been so, so good. This situation being true? Bad. Really bad.

If Lincoln learned what happened, he'd be devastated. And livid. There was no way he'd believe the truth—that she'd gone to a party and been intimate with a stranger who turned out to be Jake.

There were already insecurities and suspicions. Sasha's busy schedule, that along with full days of calling and planning had also included almost daily social lunches and enjoying dinners with Avery, Willow and Reign, had only allowed for minimal contact with her ex-fiancé, and mostly through text. He'd initially acted okay about the sporadic communication, and their breakup, and seemed to have accepted it without much resistance. Now he acted as though there'd never been a

conversation, as though they were getting ready to secure venues, interview ministers and pick out a tuxedo
and dress. She knew they needed to have another conversation. She'd rather eat an unpeeled artichoke right
now but since it was Friday night, she didn't have plans,
and the weekend would be super busy, she picked up
her phone. It rang in her hands. She looked down expecting to see Lincoln's face. Instead, a local area code
fairly pulsated from the screen.

"Hello?"

"Sasha, it's Jake."

"Jake." Immediately, an image of Zorro wearing a
mask and not much else, thrusting his strength deep inside her, wafted into Sasha's mind. Her nipples pebbled
at the thought, along with the sound of a voice that now
blended with the one heard at the party. Ardent desire
was followed by an intense longing for something that
for a few very good reasons could never be. Even once
the breakup with Lincoln was made public, she could
never tell Jake about that night. What would he think
of her? Would he judge her, question how someone engaged could sleep with a stranger? Would he be angry
that she'd caused him to accidentally sleep with his
colleague's fiancée? What would that mean for their
business venture? What would it mean if her family
found out? What if in learning the truth Jake felt betrayed and refused to date her? Or even see her again?
Those were too many what-ifs for Sasha to handle. Way
too many mines in that field of possibility to think of
anything more lasting than the Chitty Bedroom Bang
Bang she'd accidentally pulled off. A coincidence that
had crazy odds of ever happening. A mistake, a twist of

fate she'd happily unravel again and again. Stolen moments that may be a lifetime secret of hers alone. Yet one that should she die tomorrow, it would be with the memory of one time in her life being fully, incredibly and thoroughly sexually satisfied.

Sasha heard Jake repeat her name. The guy had her zoning out! "I'm sorry, what did you say?"

"I asked what you were doing?"

"Um, I'm checking emails, social media…not much. We just got back a little while ago. Val is having dinner with some of her soror sisters."

"Did you pledge?"

"No, you?"

"No."

"That's interesting."

"Why do you say that?"

"I don't know." Sasha gave a shrug that Jake couldn't see. "It's easy to imagine you barking."

"Ha! You're funny."

"Did I say that out loud?" What was it about Jake that felt so exciting? If she smiled any harder, her face might break.

"How'd you get my number?"

"TJ. He was surprised I didn't have it, being your protector and all."

"I'm surprised he called you when he knew Lincoln would."

"Looks like there's a lot of interest in you and Lincoln tying the knot, in you not getting away."

"Unfortunately, you're right."

"Hope you don't mind. About my getting your number, that is."

"As long as you don't turn into a stalker blowing up my phone." *And as long as you don't turn out to be Zorro, although I already know that you are.*

"I don't make promises I might not be able to keep."

Sasha chuckled. "Now who's got jokes?"

There was a companionable silence before Jake continued. "You said Val was going out for dinner. What are you going to do?"

"Probably have something delivered. It's been a packed week. I might turn it into a night of Netflix and chill."

"Not alone. That's not allowed."

Sasha knew she couldn't invite Jake to Val's house. Her resolve would go out the window. She'd have him naked and shagging her in five minutes flat.

"Then why don't you come over and take me someplace nice?"

"Look at the modern woman asking me out on a date."

"I suggested dinner. As my protector. Didn't think it was a big deal since we've both got to eat."

"It's no big deal."

"Good. Val has shown me quite of bit of your quaint town, but I haven't seen much of Chicago."

"This your first visit to Chicago?"

"I've been here a few times, but that was years ago when I was a kid."

"What's your favorite cuisine?"

"Cooked. Tasty."

"I think that can be managed. But nothing fancy. I'm tired, and don't feel like being social. This week's been a beast."

"Why didn't you say so? We don't have to go out. I was only half-serious when I made the suggestion."

"Don't try and back out now. We've decided. Throw on a pair of jeans and I'll be there in thirty."

"I guess you know Val's address."

His voice lowered suggestively. "I know everything."

She laughed airily and hung up the phone, as though what he'd said hadn't brought goose bumps. No telling what Jake would do if he discovered her secret about the tryst they'd likely shared. Or how TJ would react or what Lincoln would think, let alone the rest of her family.

She got off the couch and headed to her bedroom with the hope that the details of her first night in Chicago would remain a secret. Twenty minutes later she was showered and dressed, grateful for Jake's suggestion to make it a casual night. She wore a favorite pair of skinny jeans decorated with a spray of white crystals. A few of the same type crystals also decorated an oversize black sweater that paired perfectly with a pair of flat suede ankle boots. She'd forgotten to pack the signature scent she'd been wearing the night of the party but had snagged a bottle of Artsy by Kimberly New York from Val's extensive collection. She sprayed her temples, wrist and the cleavage beneath her sweater, then finished her look with silver hoops and a few thin bangles. Minimal makeup gave off a fresh-faced appearance that worked perfectly with a high ponytail. Having achieved what she hoped was a look that conveyed "sexy but not trying," Sasha grabbed her phone, purse and headed toward the hall closet to retrieve her coat. When the phone rang as she reached for it, she assumed it was Jake. She was about to ask if he was outside and almost fainted when instead of his number she saw Lincoln's face. She sent a thank-you to the angels who'd saved that faux pas.

"Lincoln, hi. I've been meaning to call." Putting the call on Speaker, she set her coat and purse on a foyer table and walked to a window.

"I guess you're pretty busy."

He was upset. Sasha could hear it in his tone and didn't totally blame him. She'd been gone for a week. They'd only talked once and then for less than five minutes. Before they were exes they were friends who talked almost every day.

"It's been a whirlwind. Lots of adjusting. I'm sorry for not having had more time to talk."

"So tell me all about Chicago, or rather where you're staying, Point..."

"Point du Sable. It's beautiful, actually. Very upscale. Think Prince George energy squeezed into a much smaller location."

"What's there to do in a small town that's got you so busy?"

"Oh, Val has quite the social calendar. My first day here I went to an Eddington brunch and made some new friends."

"I recently read an article in *Forbes* about their company. I have to admit their business models are progressive, real cutting-edge. I was impressed. Even more so that when Jake and I discussed our possible business venture, he wasn't all braggadocious about it. You talked to him, right?"

"Jake? Yes, we talked. He was at the brunch."

"Good. With him around to keep an eye out, I feel more comfortable with you being there."

"Have you forgotten about our breakup? That I'm not your responsibility anymore?"

"Don't be silly, Sasha. You'll always be my responsibility."

At the end of that road was an argument. Sasha decided to make a verbal turn.

"One of the executive's wives owns an event planning business. Her name is Avery. I had lunch with her this week, and another woman who works for her."

"What about the other men?"

The question caught her off guard. She recovered quickly. "The Eddington brothers?"

"Anybody you've met who I might have to check and let them know you're not available."

Rather than fight, Sasha decided to go along. "Relax, Lincoln. All of the guys I met are well taken. I met Maeve, one of Jake's sisters, and her husband, Victor. He's a hotshot lawyer practicing between Chicago and his Costa Rican hometown. Avery's husband is named Cayden. He's not an Eddington but seems to be treated like a part of their family."

"Yeah, he's a tech guy. Created an app that changed how a lot of companies do business." He paused and then, "There weren't any single guys at the brunch?"

"Why? Are you looking for a single guy?"

A snort followed her attempt at humor and any second chance of lightening the moment was interrupted by a ringing doorbell.

"Oh, that's…that's my ride." Sasha hurried to get off the phone. "I'm going to grab a bite to eat. Talk later?"

"Sure. Who's taking you out?"

"Jake. My protector," she added, as a cushion to soften any potential blow.

"You're going out with Jake Eddington?"

The doorbell rang again.

"Hang on, Linc."

She muted the call and opened the door. Jake stood there smiling, looking like the tasty meal she'd earlier described.

"Hey." The breathy greeting wasn't intended. "You could have just texted to let me know you were here."

Jake looked aghast. "If my dad heard something like that about one of his sons, he'd pitch a fit." He reached for her arm. "You look nice."

"Thanks."

They headed for a sporty pearl-white number that oozed luxury and good taste. Jake opened the door and noted her phone. "You talking to someone?"

"Oh, shoot. I forgot." She slid into one of the softest seats her butt had ever encountered and unmuted her phone. "Sorry about that. I had to answer the door. Let's talk later, okay?"

"Is that Jake?"

"Yes."

"Remember, Sasha, we're still engaged."

"We're just grabbing a bite to eat. I'll call you later." Her finger tapping the End Call button served as goodbye.

Jake had entered the car midconversation. He advised her to buckle up and drove out of the cul-de-sac before speaking.

"Trouble in paradise?"

"It's…never mind."

"Sometimes it feels better to talk things out."

In that moment Sasha wanted nothing more than to talk to Jake. To spill her guts and tell him everything, about the breakup and more, like what she'd endured while attending boarding school but never told anyone. Incidents that rocked her self-esteem and confidence, so much so that as a grown-ass woman she'd hide a breakup from her parents, which more resembled the actions of a child. She wanted to come clean with how she'd lied about not being at the party and how she'd had the best sex ever, accidentally with him, and how she wasn't promiscuous or a slut—no really—but she'd absolutely positively like to do it again. Soon. Tonight. She wanted to say all of this. But she didn't. Even worse she wasn't sure there would ever be a good time to have such conversations.

"Having second thoughts about getting married?"

Sasha's head whipped around. "What made you ask that?"

"Your reaction when questioned the other day, for one. That phone call for another." He nodded his head toward her bare hand. "You not wearing a ring."

Sasha held up her hand as though it were a foreign object being seen for the first time. "I forget," was the excuse that sounded lame to her ears.

Time to change the subject.

"Where are we going?"

"A cool hole-in-the-wall on the city's south side. Beer on tap, the wine red or white and some of the best chicken wings and sides on the planet." He glanced over. "Think you can handle that?"

Remembering his earlier quip, she mimicked, "I can handle everything."

Sasha couldn't remember when she'd had such a great time. The eatery felt like a neighborhood club. Everybody knew Jake, who was treated like a pro sports guru. The music was a fun mixture of 2000s' classics from the worlds of pop, hip-hop and R & B. He hadn't lied. The wings were delicious, with so many choices. Sasha tried a half dozen different kinds and washed it all down with a no-name white wine. Jake was a cool guy, naturally capturing center stage. They never lacked for conversation. He was well-traveled and -read. Like Willow, he spoke fluent French. Unlike either woman, because of his brother-in-love, Victor, Jake spoke Spanish almost fluently too. Even so, he conversed with the regulars as though he'd grown up in their neighborhood. Sasha was surprised to find herself feeling completely at home there. At one point she thought of her family and imagined her father's face upon seeing her at such an establishment. The visual made her laugh out loud.

"What's funny, now?"

Sasha reached for a napkin to wipe her Thai-sauce-stained fingers. "I just thought about my father. I love the food and the vibe but if my bougie parents knew I was here they'd have a heart attack."

Jake took a swig of beer. "I can see that."

"How'd you find it?"

"There's a Boys & Girls Club a few blocks over. My dad used to mentor there. I'd often go with him. It's where I met Cayden. We hung out here all the time."

"So, this place has been around since you were a kid?"

"Owned by the same family for generations, with a menu that gets updated, but the basics never change."

"Thanks for bringing me here. Back home I hardly ever…there are a lot of expectations. With my dad so visible on the Hill there is always a spotlight. Appearance is everything. I always feel on." She used air quotes to emphasize the last word. "This has been a refreshing change. I can't remember the last time I… just…thanks."

"Think nothing of it. Not only is the food delicious but it makes for a cheap date." Jake stood and threw a few bills on the table. "Let's get out of here."

Outside he slipped more money to two young teens who'd agreed to watch his car, then more to a man who seemed down on his luck. Sasha silently watched these exchanges, knowing innately that this wasn't for show. It was who he was.

"You're generous."

He looked at her before leaving the curb. "I can afford to be."

"I know a lot of rich people who don't give back."

"Let's make sure that's never us." Jake reached for her hand and for whatever reason she didn't pull back. The moment felt authentic and right. He felt right, the same as her Zorro did at the party that night. With a final squeeze he removed his hand and with it the blanket of tranquility over the evening. After feeling her phone vibrate, she reached into her purse to check it. There were missed calls from Lincoln, and TJ, and her mom. She slipped the phone back into her purse and gazed out the window.

"Everything okay?"

"Yes."

Except it wasn't.

On the drive back to Point du Sable, music replaced the earlier lively conversation. Thankfully, Jake left her alone with her thoughts. When they reached Val's home he pulled into the drive and kept the car running while coming around to open the passenger door. They were quiet on the short walk to the home's front entrance. Sasha hated for the night to end.

"Thanks again, Jake. That was so much fun."

He nodded but didn't respond. Instead, he kissed her forehead and pulled her into a warm embrace. She could feel his pounding heartbeat and imagined hers was beating just as fast. With a sigh he released her and stepped back.

"Let's get you inside, make sure you're safe before I go."

Sasha placed a thumb on the sensor. The door opened with a soft whoosh.

"See you later," she offered once inside.

He stood for a moment longer, hands pushed into pockets, then returned to his car. She watched her secret lover stroll over and get in. After observing his face and watching those sexy lips all night, there was no longer any doubt in her heart. Jake Eddington was her Zorro. As she watched his disappearing taillights from the window, Sasha got the uneasy yet anticipatory feeling that life as she had known it until that point was also quickly fading.

Six

Jake had just stepped into his office in preparation for a video conference call when his cell phone rang. He glanced at his watch and tapped the phone's face to take a call from someone he wanted to talk to but currently didn't have time for.

"Linc! I was going to call you later. Right now, I've got five minutes. What's up?"

The briefest of pauses before the response. "That's what I called to find out. What's up with you and Sasha?"

The question didn't take Jake by surprise. He'd been expecting this call since Friday night when he'd heard Sasha's side of the conversation with her fiancé. The tone surprised him, though. Lincoln was the one who'd asked him to look after Sasha. Now he had an attitude about it? Sure, he was attracted to his friend's fiancée. Any red-blooded man like him would appreciate a woman like her. But Jake never cheated. He never played second fiddle. He didn't break up relationships. He was also an excellent poker player. All of these thoughts were kept to himself as he spoke with a smile in his voice.

"Just keeping an eye on her, man, as you asked."

"That's all you're keeping on her...an eye?"

"Lincoln. We've known each other for years and might become business partners. If there is a question you want to ask or a comment you want to make, do it. Quickly. I've got a meeting to lead."

"Fine. How much time are you spending with Sasha?"

The smile faded. He worked to keep the growing impatience he felt from his tone.

"Not much. I saw her the day she arrived and attended our family brunch. And this past Friday, we had dinner together. Not a date, just a meal. She was talking to you when I picked her up, which is probably what led to your suspicions and this call."

Lincoln didn't respond immediately. Jake checked his watch again. "I'm late for a conference call. Let's finish this another time."

"Fine. But you should know something about my fiancée. Sasha is brilliant but she can also be flighty. Impulsive. Taking action without thinking things through. A lot of that is my fault. And her family. Her parents and brothers. Her being the only girl, we were all overly protective. I've known her nearly all my life. We kept her sheltered, which means she doesn't always have the experience necessary to make the right decisions. It's one of the reasons I asked you to look out for her.

So she wouldn't be taken advantage of by one of those smooth-talking Chicago brothers with a world of promises and a fat bank account."

"From what I've seen during the brief times Sasha and I have spent together, you may be underestimating what she is capable of. That's my opinion, for what it's worth."

"You don't know Sasha. I do. I just want to make sure that I haven't made a mistake and asked the fox to guard the henhouse."

"I'm a man of integrity, Lincoln, who would never intentionally do anything to hurt either of you, or myself. That said, I've got to run. Talk to you, later."

Fortunately, Jake didn't have time to immediately reflect on the conversation. Had that been the case he would probably have been pissed. Instead, he set down his phone and fired up his computer screen just as his assistant opened the meeting app. For the next forty minutes, his mind was engaged in sports and two potential clients currently living in Atlanta. Both looked to be solid candidates for the types of portfolios he liked to manage. After giving an overview of the company's unique investment methods and answering a barrage of questions, he agreed to fly south that weekend for a personal meeting. He spent the rest of the day monitoring stocks and researching start-up tech and AI companies, often great vehicles from which to help his client's money grow. That evening he had dinner with his older brother, Desmond, who along with several other American-company executives had just returned from fact-finding missions to Africa and China. He learned that on both continents business was booming, some of which dovetailed with his desire to focus his clients on companies involved in technology, especially organic biotech. It had been a long yet productive day, with almost twelve hours passing from the time he talked to Linc and the chance he got to speak with Sasha later that night. After taking a shower and changing into a pair of comfy sweats, he kicked back in his favorite lounge chair, used his remote to turn the music on low and called her.

"Hey, gorgeous," he said when she answered, his voice taking on a husky quality that was totally unplanned.

"Hi, Jake."

Said with no flirtation at all, which caused Jake to straighten a bit, and further turn down the volume on the channel of contemporary jazz.

"Linc called you?"

"How'd you know that?"

"Because he phoned me as well. I was headed into a meeting but we spoke for a few minutes."

"And?"

"He seems worried about the state of your relationship—overly concerned if you ask me. Which you didn't."

"What did he say?"

"Asked me how much time we were spending together, basically if we were seeing each other."

He heard Sasha make a sound of frustration. "Linc sometimes gets insecure and possessive. I have always been a free bird and even in a soul mate relationship want to continue to fly. It's just…never mind. I'm sorry you got dragged into this."

"I don't mind. Lincoln called and asked me to look out for you. I guess I was involved already."

Jake eased off the lounge chair and walked barefoot into the kitchen. He opened the fridge and gazed at the contents, unsure of what he wanted.

"Can I ask you a question?"

"You can ask."

"It's personal, so feel free to tell me it's none of my business." He grabbed a bottle of sparkling water, closed the fridge and continued to the master suite.

"Are you in love with the guy? With Linc?"

The pause was so long he wasn't sure that she'd answer. "It's…"

"Complicated?" he finished when she didn't. "That's a common description."

"Relationships aren't always easy."

"Care to explain?"

Sasha softly cleared her throat. "It's hard to talk about."

"I get that. Might be helpful, though."

Again, she hesitated. "Promise it stays between us?"

"Of course."

Jake didn't want to have this conversation lying down. He crossed over to a stationary bike that hadn't been used in months and began pedaling slowly.

"Okay." She took a breath. "Lincoln and I have known each other practically all our lives. I can't remember a time without him. Our fathers and mothers are the best of friends. For several years, we were neighbors during our summers spent in Sag Harbor."

"How did they meet, your parents and his?"

"Our mothers went to Spelman. Lincoln's dad, Elijah, went to Morehouse, so he's known Mother since their college years."

"You call your mom Mother?" Jake asked.

"Yes."

"Isn't that a bit formal?"

"When discussing them casually it's mom and dad but when addressed, it's what they prefer.

"Anyway, my dad went to Brown and met my mom shortly after graduation, when she was doing an internship on Capitol Hill."

"I didn't know your mom was into politics like that."

"Mother was into securing a socially appropriate husband. Actually, more specifically, that was Grandmother's plan. The senator Mom interned for was a friend of the family. Anyway, the plan worked. Mom met Dad fairly quickly. When they got married, Lincoln's mom, Ruthanne, was my mom's maid of honor, which is how dad and her husband met. Mother and Ruthanne's close friendship led to the men eventually becoming close as well."

"And the children, once families began."

"Yep."

"And then you and Lincoln went from being friends to dating," Jake said, drawing out the sentence for emphasis.

"I think our mothers always held a secret hope that we'd get together. Looking back, I can see little things they did over the years to push the two of us in that direction. Parties, society dances, vacations, stuff like that. Once I left for boarding school, Lincoln would get together with a few of his friends and come over to Switzerland to visit. He always wanted to go to Brown, like my dad, and talked me into going there too. By the time I returned to attend college in Rhode Island, being a couple just felt like the right thing to do."

Jake stopped pedaling, rubbing his chin in contemplation. "That's a cool history, actually," he said, and meant it. "There's a very important word, though, that's missing from the story. The word that brings me back to my first question. Do you love him?"

"Not in the way that he deserves from the woman who'll bear his last name."

"Then why are you doing it? Why get married to someone who feels more like a good friend than a husband?"

"I'm not."

She'd spoken so softly, Jake was sure he'd misunderstood.

"Come again?"

"Jake, seriously, what I'm about to tell you can't be shared with anyone. Lincoln is the only one who knows."

"Don't worry." Jake began slowly pedaling the stationary bike again. "This conversation remains just between us."

"Lincoln and I are no longer engaged. We broke things off before I came here."

Pedaling ceased. He took a sip of water while absorbing what she'd said. Sasha's bad news shouldn't have made Jake feel good…but it did. "Then why are you acting like you're still together?"

"He asked to wait until after the holidays before making the breakup official. I agreed because, quite frankly, telling my family what's happened scares me to death."

"They might be disappointed, but don't you think they'll understand?"

"Not really. We've already had the engagement party. It was an intimate gathering, but people know."

"Yes, but they'd have to support you. The family, I mean. Your happiness is most important, after all."

"If that were the case, they'd know already. But it isn't. In my family, perception is everything. Scandal is worse than death. My change of heart will cause embarrassment, for both families, and gossip in a society circle where both my mom and Ruthanne thrive. Honestly, even now, I don't know if I'll be able to do it, go through with my plans to end it."

"Want to know what I think?"

"No, but I think you're going to tell me."

It did Jake's heart good to hear a smile in her voice. It was the first light moment all night.

"What do you think?"

"I think that you marrying someone to make others happy is a mistake. A move that wouldn't be fair to anyone. Not to you. Not to your family. Not to Linc."

"You're right, but as you said earlier, this really isn't your business."

The comment rubbed Jake the wrong way. In ways that made no sense it felt as though Sasha was his concern. He gritted his teeth against a sudden outburst. When he spoke, his voice was calm.

"Before you came to the Point, your fiancé and your brother TJ asked me to look out for you. I told them I would. That made it my business. Given how beautiful, intelligent and captivating you are it is totally understandable why he'd be concerned."

"Linc's and my brother's actions are for the little girl they remember who went off to Switzerland. They have yet to recognize who I am right now. I've tried to make it clear that the little girl is now her own woman but they see who they want to see."

"I believe Linc sees the woman he wants to marry."

"As I said, Linc and I practically grew up together. We love each other. But that type of love is not enough. He is a strategist with a very specific life direction. I'm still figuring mine out."

"Exactly. That's when it's important to slow things down, be able to listen and clearly see what's around you."

"Is that so?"

"Yes, it is."

"Then since you're such a relationship expert, let's talk about your love life. Who are you seeing, and where does marriage fit into your future?"

An image flashed in Jake's mind. A tiger mask. A woman's nearly naked body bathed in moonlight. A dragonfly tattoo glistening with sweat. His sex began to harden at the memory.

"What? All of a sudden the cat's got your tongue?"

A jolt hit Jake's heart. *A cat indeed.* "Nothing serious, though there is this one woman…"

"What about her?"

"A few weeks ago, we hooked up at a party. Had some mutually casual adult fun. There was something there. We just…clicked, you know?"

Silence followed, each in their own world. "Did you… I mean…are the two of you dating?"

Sasha's voice was tentative. But Jake didn't notice, preoccupied as he was in his own thoughts.

"I want to date her. But it was a masquerade party.

I couldn't tell you what she looks like. I mean, she was beautiful, but we were both wearing masks. It's a damn shame to say out loud, but I don't even know her name. I asked. She wouldn't tell me."

"Oh."

"I haven't given up on finding her, though. There was something special about her."

"That you're still thinking about her weeks later means she made quite an impression."

"Not saying if I saw her I'd bend the knee and propose, but yeah, she was impressive. If I ever do get married, I want it to be to a person who captivates me, like she did. Not just to somebody I *like*, who I've known forever, who is a 'good friend of the family.'"

The conversation shifted after that. They talked sports, Val's holiday drive, Sasha going home for Thanksgiving. They ended the call with Jake's thoughts focused not on Sasha, but on the mystery tigress he told her about. He wasn't sure why he'd even mentioned her, except Sasha was a good listener, and easy to talk to. It was the first time he'd shared what happened that night with anyone. Doing so reignited his determination to uncover his pussycat's identity, and once again take that sexy tiger by the tail.

Seven

Sasha pushed away from the desk where she'd been trying to focus on a speech Val had written and wanted her to read. *Trying* being the operative word. She got up, stretched and walked over to the window to catch some of the bright afternoon sun. And think. Since the revelation that Jake was Zorro, and their conversation a few days later, the secret lover had constantly been on her mind. What he'd said about her, how he felt.

There is this one woman...

There was something there. We just...clicked...

I want to date her... There was something special...

That he'd been talking to said mystery woman and didn't know it was driving her to distraction! Trying to figure out a way to come clean about that night without him getting angry or feeling betrayed had kept her up at night. That and the fact that the more time she talked to or spent time with Jake since being in Point du Sable, the more her feelings grew. Before, it had been an attraction nursed through an imagined sense of who he was based on infrequent passings, his internet image and snippets of news. Now it was knowing how compatible they were—physically, mentally—how well they clicked, as he'd said.

It was horrible to compare the two men but Sasha couldn't help it. The Sunday after dining with Jake, Sasha had called Lincoln. They'd managed a cordial conversation, almost as comfortable as old times. He hadn't asked about Jake. Rather, had kept the focus on them as a couple—trips, concerts, things they'd done together. Clearly, in his mind they were still a pair. Sasha was equally sure that the relationship was over. She felt guilty about that, but the truth could not be denied. Jake was everything that Lincoln was not. Jake was super intelligent with swagger to burn. He was funny, sexy, a man who showed strength without being macho. Lincoln wasn't chopped liver. He just wasn't… Jake. He hoped their relationship could be rekindled. She knew that couldn't happen, not feeling about Jake as she did. To marry one man while being in love with another would be fifty shades of wrong.

Wait, was she in love?

Sasha decided it was much too early for the *L* word. She chalked the thought snafu to being stressed over the event, the holidays, Lincoln and undoubtedly at some point their families coming together. There was still a week to go until that happened, which meant there was still time here in the Point to spend with Jake. To make him feel about her the way he felt about…well…her. After hours of overthinking, Sasha decided it was all too much to handle on her own. She needed help. But who to call? She paced back and forth from the living room to the fireplace to the foyer and back. Midway through the third pass it came to her. Reign. Of course. Sasha couldn't believe she hadn't thought of her sooner. She sent a text. Reign called her back and within the hour they'd made plans to meet for lunch the next day. That matter settled, Sasha was able to get through Val's speech, tweak certain areas for emphasis and make long overdue phone calls to her mom and dad. Restless after those conversations, she borrowed the car Valencia kept stored at her mom's house, fired up the GPS and headed to Chicago. Nothing like a good shopping spree to cure whatever ailed you. Her therapy took place along the Magnificent Mile. Marcus. Bloomingdale's. Nordstrom. Cartier. Sasha returned to Point du Sable loaded down with packages and feeling good as new. That night was the best sleep ever!

The next day, she dressed in one of her designer finds—a wine-colored front-wrap jumpsuit that she matched with a favorite pair of leather boots, dangly earrings and a clunky wooden bracelet she'd found at T.J.Maxx. Breakfast consisted of a bagel and tea, before meeting with Val and the ladies at the country club to flesh out the evening program that would mark the official end of the drive. She drove around town for a bit, partly to see how well she could navigate it without GPS (not very well, it turned out), but mostly to kill time. Finally, she hit the highway for the short twenty-minute drive into Chicago and the café Reign had suggested for their one o'clock lunch. It was another sunny day, so much so that the chilly thirty-seven-degree temperature barely registered. She entered the cozy, bohemian-styled establishment and spotted Reign immediately.

"Don't you look runway ready," she teased, after the ladies shared a hug and sat. "Is that leather and mohair?"

Reign nodded.

"That is so cool. Where'd you get it?"

"I think, Dubai."

"Of course it would be from somewhere requiring a passport and a transatlantic flight."

The server came over with lemon water and menus. She sported a huge afro and piercings, a perfect fit for the scene.

"Chicago has such cool restaurants."

"I've enjoyed a few in DC," Reign replied. "I try to get by Busboys and Poets whenever I'm in town."

"I love that place. A good friend of mine, Carol Cooper, works with the artists. Do you have any of their work?"

"No, and given how much I appreciate the art on their walls that is totally embarrassing."

"No problem. I've got you. Next time you're in DC, I'll hook you up."

"Cool."

Sasha scanned the menu. "Everything on the menu is vegan? I know you told me that, but…"

Reign laughed. "Don't worry. I get that a lot. Guaranteed, you'll love everything they make. The owner, Qiana, is a personal friend and I'm in love with the chef's skills. He could cook a shoe and you'd eat it."

"Are you one hundred percent vegan?"

"No, I'm not quite ready for that. I love seafood too much. And meat."

The ladies enjoyed a laugh as they placed their orders. The server delivered their teas. Sasha took a sip and was immediately smitten.

"Okay, they should sell this by the gallon. Thanks so much for agreeing to meet me today. I know you're busy."

"Your timing was perfect. I was glad you called because I was going to call you. I've felt bad about not being able to spend more time with you since you got here."

"Val has kept me busy. Who knew collecting and giving away food, toys and clothes could get so complicated?"

"It can when done on the scale that Mrs. Baldwin likes to do it."

"I have no complaints. Everyone here has been very welcoming, and Val is one of my favorite people in the world."

"Your godmother, right?" Sasha nodded. "It's very generous of you to come all this way and spend so much time to help her. Especially being engaged and probably planning a wedding. What does your fiancé think about that?"

It was Reign's brother, not Lincoln, that Sasha went there to discuss. Still, Sasha entertained the question. "He's not happy."

"Has he been out to visit?"

"He works a lot."

"What does he do?"

"He's a consultant, and entrepreneur. In fact, he and Jake might work on a project together."

"Then all the more reason he should be able to come here for the weekend. Or an evening. From DC to Chicago isn't a long flight.

"Hey, my boyfriend's birthday is coming up. We're throwing a party. The two of you are more than welcome to come."

"That sounds fun, Reign. If I'm in town, I'd love to attend. But Linc won't be able to make it."

"Well, tell him just in case."

"Oh, hell, Reign. I might as well tell you." Sasha let out a sigh of resolve. "I've ended my engagement."

"Oh, no! And here I am going on about parties and wedding planning and weekend trips."

"It's alright."

"What happened? Never mind. You probably don't want to talk about it."

"Actually, I do. It's one of the reasons I asked you to lunch. I grew up with two hardhead brothers and could use some sisterly advice."

"Then I'm even more happy to be here having lunch with you. Speaking of, they serve liquor. Sure you don't want to make that a Chi-Town Tea?"

Sasha laughed. "No, I'm okay."

"Just double-checking. It's delicious. They blend cognac, amaretto and some other good stuff. If you're worried about driving, there's always Uber."

"I'm good," Sasha replied, with a shake of her head. "I've got some serious decisions to make and need to think clearly."

The server delivered an appetizer plate. Reign dug into a hummus trio with pita points. Sasha talked.

"Linc and I haven't been on the same page for a while. We were, well, I was just going through the motions. I love him, but as a very dear friend, not a husband. I told him that and ended the engagement. But we haven't announced it. Our families still think we're headed for marital bliss."

"Ooh, that's tough."

"It's the hardest place I've ever been."

"You think they'll be disappointed?"

"That's an understatement. Our families have been friends for decades. Lincoln and I getting married is their happily-ever-after."

"But not yours."

"Not at all."

"Then you have to tell them, Sasha. They'll get over it. What is that saying? 'To thine own self be true.'"

"Sounds easy enough when I'm here in Chicago. But when talking to my parents or brothers, just thinking of telling the truth makes me nauseous. I've always done what my parents expected, gone down the common road traveled by those of our ilk. Boarding school, debutante announcement, society clubs, college, the whole nine. I've lived a life doing what they wanted me to do instead of what I want to do. And I'm sick of it!"

Reign high-fived her. "Girl! You're preaching to the choir. I feel the same way."

"You do?"

"Well, there's not a man involved but I know what it's like to be in a demanding family with high expectations. It was expected for all of Derrick's kids to work in the company. Nothing was stated. We just knew."

"I've seen the company's commercials. Very creative. Isn't that your baby? Don't you handle PR?"

"Yes. I worked with the team on that concept and am proud with how it turned out. I don't hate what I do, but if given the option, I'd do something else."

"Like what?"

"Become a lifestyle influencer," Reign immediately answered. "With a blog or independent channel. I adore clothes—buying them, wearing them, seeing what others are wearing. I love visiting different places, different cultures and stuff. But this lunch isn't about me. It's about you. Are you sure there's no way to work out whatever's going on with your ex?"

"I'm positive that's over. Emotionally, I've already disconnected. I like someone else."

"Really?"

"Yes." Sasha swallowed her nervousness. There would be no putting this milk she was about to spill back into the bottle. "Your brother."

"Jake?"

Sasha nodded.

Reign rolled her eyes. "Girl, everybody likes Jake. Don't let him be the reason you're giving back the ring."

"Why do you say that? Is there something about him I should know? A reason not to date him, I mean, if he asked me out?"

Reign slumped against the chair and crossed her arms. "How long have y'all been talking?"

Hearing Reign's comment, the thought to discuss what happened at HalloMask now felt wrong. It was one thing for her to know about Sasha's attraction, another to learn that she'd already slept with the man. The weight of the secret was heavy within her. But Sasha wasn't ready to share a most intimate and amazing part of her life with anyone else, especially before Jake knew the truth. In formulating an answer, a ruler could not have helped Sasha better measure her words.

"We've hung out once or twice," she carefully offered. "As friends. During a conversation discussing their potential joint business venture, Linc asked Jake to look out for me."

"Then Linc must not know my brother very well. Nothing personal but he's a panty magnet. No matter the woman's status they all get charmed. Without him even trying! He has what my sister and I call the Eddington Edge."

Sasha's intimate acquaintance with that Eddington Edge almost caused her to blush.

"Look, I love my brother. He's a good man. Really, he is. But he loves the ladies and in my humble opinion is nowhere near ready to settle down. I'm not saying that's what you're looking for. I'm not telling you who to go out with. We're all adults. I'm just saying that if you're looking for long-term, Jake will most likely not be the one."

"I was just curious, that's all."

Reign reached over and grasped Sasha's hand. "Sounds like with an ex still holding on and an unknowing family, you already have a lot to handle."

"You're right."

"That may not have been what you wanted to hear."

"I wanted your advice. I appreciate it."

"But are you going to take it?"

"Maybe. Maybe not."

Reign shook her head. "I swear, my brothers and that Eddington Edge energy. I've seen it in action but I tell them it's bullshit unless there's a way that magnetism can be packaged and sold."

"Figure out a way and you'll become trillionaires."

"And Jake will finally be known for something other than running his big fat mouth!"

Sasha loved hanging out with Reign, who as much as she teased, truly loved her brother. Her choice for lunch had been spot-on. The Tasty Vegan's dishes lived up to the name. Sasha also appreciated how Reign handled the discussion about Jake. Honest in the way a friend would be. Selective in what she shared as a sister should be. Once entrées arrived, the topics steered away from her lover. By the time the check arrived, Sasha had made a decision. She had to come clean with Jake. Tell him everything. About that night at the HalloMask party. How their paths had crossed, and what happened next. What she'd wanted to keep secret but couldn't. She was the tiger he wanted to tame.

Eight

"Yo, man. Where are you? Because your mind's not here."

Jake looked over at his client and forced himself away from the text Reign had just sent, one that magnified thoughts that for days had wavered between Sasha Mc-Dowell and the HalloMask mystery lover. That he was attracted to his business colleague's off-limits girlfriend was bad enough. She'd said the engagement was off, but he couldn't be sure. Couples went on-again, off-again all the time. That he hadn't yet uncovered the tigress's identity was even more frustrating. That didn't mean the search was over. He was more motivated than ever to find her. Even if Sasha officially ended her relationship, he wouldn't feel comfortable throwing his hat in the proverbial ring. He was on the verge of launching a consulting firm independent of Eddington Enterprise, possibly with Linc. No, now wasn't the time for a train of thought that could lead nowhere. His interest lay with the tigress, not Sasha. It took effort but he returned his focus to the client sitting next to him at a private strip club.

"Sorry, Michael. What did you say?"

Michael stretched a pair of thick, heavily muscled legs into the cozy room's dollar-strewn aisle and gave Jake a speculative eye.

"Are you okay?"

"I'm fine. Why do you ask?"

"Because the finest dancer in here just passed by buck naked, and your eyes never left your cell phone. You never looked up."

Jake shrugged. "I told you before we came here. Strip clubs aren't my thing."

"And I told you they served the best steaks in the state."

"Then I say we place our orders and get on with this meeting."

"We're waiting on Levi, remember? Your soon-to-be client if all goes well, and the reason you're here?"

Jake checked his watch. "You told him six o'clock, right?"

"Yes, and it's only six fifteen. Being late is fashionable for guys like us. Besides, the night is young and the scenery is amazing. What's the rush?"

"I've got a nine o'clock flight that I don't intend to miss."

Michael produced a slow grin. "Ah, a hot date."

"Something like that. Send him a text and see if you can get an ETA."

Just then a giant of a man cast a shadow across the table. This time Jake did look up. He stood and after being introduced, shook the ginormous hand of Levi Williams, the number-one linebacker in professional football. He was also Michael's teammate and good friend. Since Levi was immediately recognized, two dancers came over to offer private performances. Levi delayed a lap dance. Michael passed. Jake returned to scrolling social media on his phone. Body Language was a high-end club, a popular spot for the rich and famous, where six- and seven-figure deals regularly went down over dinner or lunch. It was also a place that, when in town, many of Jake's clients frequented. The type of establishment that once upon a time, Jake had enjoyed. Tonight, he couldn't get into it. The meeting hadn't even started and already felt long. Still, he put on an air of professionalism, turned on the charisma and engaged in the small talk required to assuage huge egos and secure million-dollar portfolios. After ordering a round of beers and the famous porterhouses the club was known for, the men got down to business. Two hours later, Jake left with a satisfied stomach, a check for two million dollars and the trust of a young, talented football player determined to not retire from the game a millionaire and then be broke in less than five years.

The plane was delayed. It was almost midnight when Jake arrived back in Chicago. For regular folk, it might have meant the night was over. For movers and shakers like Jake, it was just getting started. He wouldn't miss Trenton's party. Not just because the baller was dating his sister, but because Reign had texted that Sasha would be there. He jumped in his car and headed straight for

Trenton's party, breaking a few laws to reach his destination in record time. Once at the rather nondescript building, he pulled his pearl-white Rolls-Royce Dawn convertible to the curb next to a waiting valet, strolled through the lobby of a boutique hotel and took the elevator to Suite 21, the penthouse turned private club that Trenton and a couple of his pro athlete friends owned. The elevator opened to a round foyer with short hallways in three directions and two intimidating bodyguards flanking the main entrance.

"Hey, Jake!" one of them greeted.

"There's the man," the other one said, as the men exchanged daps and shoulder bumps. "Your sister was looking for you."

"Thanks."

He walked down the short hall into the main room. The scene that greeted him was typical of a crowd surrounding sports stars—beautiful women, many scantily clad, and men wearing enough platinum and diamonds to equal a small country's GNP. Conversely, Jake's dress was understated. Black brushed jeans and a Boss turtleneck, a slim-line Rolex his only jewelry. A hip-hop beat pulsated beneath his feet as he gave head nods and shoulder bumps to men he knew. A brief hug or kiss on the cheek to the women. All while his eyes scanned the crowd for the face that often morphed with that of the still elusive and as-yet-unknown tigress from Halloween. He walked. And searched. And then he saw her. Perched on a bar stool. Surrounded by vultures. The very type of men he'd been tasked to help her avoid. Sasha may or may not have been a damsel in distress who needed saving, but he decided to make like a knight and be her shining armor anyway.

"Excuse me," he said, to the first back he encountered, one that belonged to a basketball player with seven more inches than the seventy-two Jake possessed.

"What's up, Jake?" There was a smile in the young man's voice. A quick nod acknowledged the star player's greeting. The question would have to wait. The brief exchange served its purpose. The men's attention was temporarily diverted from Sasha, the obvious object of their affection, and placed on to the mastermind finance guy that all of them knew. They parted as though Jake were Moses about to take a dip in the Red Sea.

Jake walked directly up to Sasha. He was not smiling.

"Hello."

"Hi," Sasha replied, with a huge grin.

"Do you have a moment? We need to talk."

His calm, brusque delivery removed the smile from her face. "What about?"

Jake looked around the room. All the booths and tables were full. Finding privacy would be difficult, but not impossible. "It's important."

She hesitated, and for a moment Jake thought she might refuse. After a few seconds she placed one and then the other cutely booted ankle on the floor before sliding off the chair. Jake tried not to be moved by the way the soft yellow furry sweater dress she wore, conservative compared to the dress of others, clung to an hourglass body and highlighted smooth flawless skin. He placed a steadying—some might say possessive—

hand beneath her elbow and guided her through a throng
of expressions that ranged from admiring to envious.

"You look very nice tonight," he murmured, while
waving to a client on the other side of the room.

"Thank you."

They reached the hallway leading to the foyer.

"Where are we going?"

"Away from this crowd, where we can talk without
shouting."

She followed him out and remained quiet until they
crossed the foyer and stepped into the hallway with
doors on either side. He checked them. All locked.

"What are you doing?"

It was a question that Jake needed to ask himself.
When he'd seen Sasha surrounded by all that talented,
wealthy testosterone, all he'd wanted to do was pull her
away. He couldn't convey all of that. Instead, he leaned
against the wall, casually crossed his arms and observed
her.

"Okay, we're away from everybody." Sasha's expression went from frowning to flirty. Jake wasn't sure
which one caused more discomfort.

She stepped dangerously close to his personal space.
One more step and she'd be in it. Two, and they could
slow dance or kiss. He preferred the latter.

"I can hear you."

His eyes narrowed. Something about her actions felt
familiar. The masked face of the tigress swam into view.
He focused on Sasha, her eyes, her lips. The smooth expanse of skin exposed by the tilt of her head. Could it
be? No. Wasn't possible. He'd asked her outright. She'd
denied it. She had not attended the HalloMask party. The

other night at the diner, the longest time they'd spent together, Sasha had been nice but never flirty. Even when he'd hugged her at Val's door, her response had been subdued. Clearly, the mystery temptress was driving him wild. That's the only reason Sasha could be reminding him so much of her right now.

"What's this about?"

He came off the wall to put distance between them. "Quite an audience you had in there."

Sasha shrugged. "Crazy how that happens at parties. You know, people gathering and talking and stuff."

"You don't want to give these guys too much attention."

Sasha's flirty manner changed. She crossed her arms in a huff. "Look, you're not my bodyguard. I thought I left that kind of scrutiny in DC."

"I told Linc I'd look out for you. And your brother. Just trying to be a man of my word."

"I'm not a kid. I don't need watching."

"Maybe not. But I know those guys. A few of them are my clients. You're just the type of beautiful woman they like."

"Jake, what's your point?"

"I just know how smooth these guys can be. I don't want you to be fooled."

"Your sister is dating an athlete. Is this what you told her?"

"I tried. She wouldn't listen."

"Sounds like a grown woman who has her own mind." Sasha's expression softened. "I appreciate that you're concerned about me. But really, I can take care of myself. I need this time to be able to relax and just be, just live, without the feeling of being monitored. Or judged. I just want to have fun, nothing serious. Nothing that comes with drama. Not that any of that is your business."

Sasha playfully sidled up against him. "You don't have to worry about anything concerning me, okay?"

That sexy smile was back. *Dammit.* And something else. The same kind of spunkiness his tigress displayed. The question was asked through similarly pouty lips. Ones that looked like they'd be better served kissing than talking. Like the tigress. He looked pointedly at her bare ring finger to be distracted from his mind's sensual musings and at the same time remind himself that even if her relationship ended with Linc, Jake couldn't date her. Not if the two men formed a business partnership. Casual acquaintances, maybe good friends, were all he and Sasha could ever be.

"Forgot your ring again, like you've forgotten you're engaged?"

Sasha gave off an impatient huff. "I told you. That's over."

"The secret breakup that aside from me, nobody knows about."

"Lincoln knows. That's the main point. And your sister."

"Maeve or Reign?"

"Reign. I don't know Maeve."

"You told her?"

Sasha nodded. "During one of our lunches."

The news pleased Jake, but it still didn't mean Sasha's actions weren't irresponsible. His growing feelings for her were inconvenient at best.

"That's all well and good but the breakup hasn't been made public. Which means if a photo of you schmoozing with a roomful of athletes got splashed across social media, it would send the wrong message. Your family would be embarrassed and to the public, Linc would look like a fool."

Sasha came toward him, stopping just inches away. "Is that why you brought me out here? To talk about my ex?"

It was a fair question. Standing here now, with her looking up at him through almond-shaped eyes framed with long lashes, her lips curved into a mischievous smile and one hand on a curvy hip, he couldn't quite remember why they were standing in the hallway instead of enjoying the festivities going on inside. At the same time, it seemed foolish to waste the moment. Why stand here talking when those cushiony lips were so close, when the cologne she wore wrapped around them like a warm breeze?

Someone else had the same idea. Before Jake could think or blink, Sasha had placed her hands on his chest, leaned into him and connected her lips with his. He closed his eyes and groaned, inwardly trying to fight the inevitable even as instinct took over. Remaining still, he allowed himself to savor the feel of her softness, noted how her breasts pressed up against him. His arms tingled with the desire to wrap themselves around her. He refrained. She swiped his lips with a timid tongue, then eased her arms around his neck as her mouth opened more fully, demanding a response. Warning bells and something else indefinable flashed in his mind. The tigress's naked body flashed across his mental screen just before he shut the thought down completely and opened his mouth to receive the gift Sasha offered.

It was like a match had been lit as a furtive meeting of pliable flesh quickly turned into a sensual dance of oral orchestration. Their tongues swirled and pressed against each other, easily, effortlessly, as though this was not the first time. Of their own accord, Jake's hands came up to grasp her arms before sliding beyond them to cup a fluffy round booty that felt even softer encased in cashmere. She moaned and shifted her head, outlined his lips with her tongue before diving back in to continue the duel. Jake slid a hand from her butt to her waist, his destination being the nipple he felt hardening against his sweater. He was almost there, had just palmed what he suspected was a nice C-cup, when a nearby burst of laughter shattered the lust-induced veil. He placed a hand on each of her shoulders, and set her gently yet determinedly away.

This woman kisses like the tigress. Feels like the woman who made sweet love. Except that was simply not possible. It couldn't have happened. Sasha and that frisky feline couldn't be the same girl.

"What are you doing?" The question came out harsher than intended. Given how her flushed skin and kiss-swollen lips made his dick jump, it was the best he could do.

Sasha seemed shaken as well. Her breasts rose and fell, riding the deep breaths she took. "I'm sorry."

She no longer reminded him of the bold tigress who'd enticed him into a room. She sounded like the vulnerable, shy, inexperienced girl Linc warned him about and her brothers protected.

"Are you trying to drive me crazy?"

"I don't know what came over me. It just…happened."

"Are you going to blame it on the alcohol?"

"I would if I'd been drinking."

"You haven't?"

She shook her head. "Reign offered a car service, but I drove myself over. And I never drink and drive."

Jake closed his eyes briefly, worked to slow the rhythm of his breathing even as he determined to lighten the moment.

"Are you saying the intoxication is from merely being in my presence?" The question came with a smirk of a smile.

"Absolutely!"

He tried to hold a neutral expression but couldn't. They both broke out in relieved laughter.

"Come on. Let's get back to the party. But know I'm going to be keeping an eye on you. We don't want anything like what took place just now to happen with any other hardhead in the room."

He reached for her hand as though it was the most natural thing to do. They turned the corner. She slid her hand out of his and wrapped an arm around his waist. He eased an arm around her shoulder and gave it an affectionate squeeze. Just as they reached the foyer, the elevator opened. They continued into the hallway leading into the main room, paying no attention to the partygoers coming from outside. Before reaching the end of the hallway, they disengaged. But not before Jake again reached for her hand and kissed it…just because.

"Sasha?"

Jake slowed to turn but Sasha hissed, "Keep walking."

They entered the main room. Sasha moved as though the devil was nipping at her heels. Even with a good six to seven inches on her in height, Jake had to lengthen his stride just to keep up. He opened his mouth to ask where the fire was when the answer came from behind him.

"Sasha! Wait!"

Jake watched Sasha's face drop for a second, pasting on a half smile before turning around.

"Hey, girl! I thought that was you."

When Sasha didn't immediately respond, she continued. "It's Chrissie! Chrissie Moore. I know it's been a minute but you couldn't have forgotten me. Kentucky Derby, two years ago. Hat so big it could have doubled for a beach shade?"

Finally, Sasha smiled. "Chrissie, hi."

She leaned in to accept the hug Chrissie offered and added, "What are you doing here?"

Chrissie looked from Jake to Sasha. Her demeanor dimmed a bit. "I was going to ask you the same thing."

"I'm helping my godmother with a holiday event. What about you?"

"I live here. Moved last year after landing a job at McCormick Place."

"Oh. Nice."

"The convention center."

"I've heard of it."

Chrissie gave Jake another long look. "Where's Lincoln?"

"In DC."

"I thought the two of you were engaged."

"Don't worry," Jake smoothly interrupted, effortlessly mesmerizing her with the Eddington Effect, basically kryptonite for women. "Linc and I are business associates. He charged me with making sure his fiancée makes it back safely." He held out his hand. "Jake Eddington."

Her eyes widened in recognition as she accepted the handshake. "Eddington Enterprise."

"One and the same."

Chrissie's countenance changed as she gave him her full attention. "I've worked with your company—well, indirectly. Your sister Maeve was one of my first McCormick Place clients. She met with us to discuss our hosting an international conference of lawyers. It ended up being virtual instead."

"It's a pleasure to meet you."

"Likewise. How do you know Reign? She's my other sister and a host for this party."

"I don't know her. I'm the plus-one of a friend who works in the Bulls' front office." She began looking around. "I think I've already lost her."

"Then we'll leave you to your search." He placed a hand on Sasha's shoulder to lead her away. "Have fun."

"Wait, Sasha. Are you going home for Thanksgiving?"

"Yes."

"Good. Mom and I are spending it with the Trotters. I'm sure we'll see you there." She leaned over and gave Sasha a half-hearted hug.

"See you later."

Jake reached for Sasha's hand. She refused it. "Let's go upstairs. It'll be less crowded up there."

"Fine but…don't do that."

"Don't be paranoid, Sasha. She knows I'm with you at Linc's request."

They took the circular staircase to the second level and continued straight ahead to a sitting room where a glass wall framed a stunning view of downtown Chicago and Lake Michigan beyond it. They walked over and stood with their backs to the door. Only then did Jake feel Sasha somewhat relax.

"I think she saw us."

"Of course she did. We just had a whole conversation."

"I mean earlier. When we were…making out in the foyer."

"She maybe saw my arm around you. Or me kiss your hand. Friends do that all the time."

"We weren't hugging and kissing like friends do," Sasha said, becoming upset. "The one time I let my guard down to try and just be myself, I run into one of Linc's family members."

"Do you think she'll say something?"

"I think that by the time this party is over, Lincoln will know everything she even thought she saw, including what we're wearing, right down to our shoes."

"It might not be that bad."

"It's bad. I can feel it. When the family gets together, the time I've spent in Point is likely to get more carved up than the Thanksgiving turkey."

"Maybe you should consider spending the holiday here, with Val. Or my family."

"That sounds tempting but my parents wouldn't hear of it. You guys would likely find a troop of McDowells and Trotters on your doorstep, ready to explode."

"We'd be okay with that. Eddingtons don't run from fires. We run into them."

Nine

Sasha didn't have to wait until Thanksgiving. The fall-out began at six o'clock the next morning. First it was a call from Lincoln, which she ignored. She fully expected a text to follow. He didn't disappoint.

Are you still with Jake? Chrissie saw the two of you at a party last night. She told me everything. You'd better not be seeing him. If Jake betrayed our trust, your parents and brothers will be disappointed. His reputation will be ruined. I'll make sure of that.

Sasha rolled over, placed a pillow over her head and tried to go back to sleep. She tossed, turned and managed to catch a wink or two before the phone rang again. This time it was TJ. Knowing that the queries would keep coming until she answered, she reached for the phone.

"It's too early for good morning, brother. What do you want?"

"Yeah, I hear you had a late night."

"I got a text from Linc after running into Chrissie last night. I knew she'd go spouting off at the mouth."

"Sounds like she had good reason."

Sasha fluffed her pillows against the headboard and sat against them. "What? That I was at a party with Jake?"

"Not just there but…acting inappropriately. Her exact words to Linc."

"Whatever."

A lame comeback, but Sasha couldn't think of anything else to say. If a public make-out session was inappropriate behavior then she and Jake were guilty as charged. But there was no way Chrissie could have seen them around the corner. Their elevator didn't arrive until Jake and Sasha were away from the location of their lust-filled crime and headed back into the party. So what had Chrissie really seen? Nothing inappropriate, nothing scandalous. At least that was the story Sasha was going to stick to.

"Is she lying? The two of you weren't fooling around?"

"We were joking around. Maybe he touched me—a hand on a shoulder, a casual hug. So what? Chrissie needs to get out of my business and find some of her own."

"What about Lincoln? He says he phoned you last night and got voice mail. And that you didn't call back or respond to his text. Does he need to get out of your business too?"

"Yes, brother. And so do you."

Next, Sasha did something for the first time in life. She hung up on her big brother, the one her parents had defined as both protector and guide. She immediately felt guilty but strangely liberated too. So much so that she rolled over and went back to sleep. This time, soundly. When her alarm went off two hours later, she saw a missed call from her mom. No surprise there; she knew it was coming. She also knew that her parents had already discussed the situation before getting her input, and that her mother and Ruthanne had probably conversed as well. For a moment she was that insecure teen ready to do anything to avoid conflict, or that would bring embarrassment or shame on the family. Memories of the bullying she endured at boarding school for the first three years, where she'd adopted and perfected the go-along-to-get-along mentality that had kept her life mostly drama free, engulfed her. While taking a shower and getting dressed for her meeting with a major food chain, she thought about all the times she changed her mind or did an action because of what someone else wanted. She wanted this time to be different. But did she have the strength to go against her family? And Lincoln's?

Not wanting to have the cloud over her head all day, she climbed into Val's daughter's car and eased out of the garage. As soon as she'd set the GPS and was on the highway heading to Chicago, she called her mom.

"Hello, Sasha."

"Hello, Mother. I see I missed your call."

"Yes, I called about an hour ago."

"I've been busy and the workday continues. I have a meeting with a grocery chain who may donate a thousand full bags and another thousand gift cards to Val's drive. Thought I'd call you back while on the way."

"Then I'll get straight to the point, Sasha. I heard some disturbing news this morning and am sure hoping that the deliverers of said news got something wrong."

Even though it was a tactic with which she was familiar, hearing the disappointment in her mother's voice made Sasha's heart fall. But Sasha knew it was past time to hold her own with her family and show them the strong, confident woman the rest of the world already knew, the one who'd expanded Val's annual toy, food and clothing drive to include long-term, life-sustaining programs. Like the ten-week workshop offered along with the food bags that would focus on nutrition, urban gardening and home-cooked, plant-based meals. Or the makeup and styling sessions, Etiquette 101 and step-by-step guidance to creating online businesses available to anyone receiving the clothing and wanting to improve their life status or raise self-esteem. Because of a suggestion inspired by Desmond's wife, Ivy, there was a strong emphasis on educational toys. Sasha made sure that along with dollhouses and skateboards, children would find positive-image books, iPads and laptops filled with educational videos, games and brain food exercises beneath the Christmas tree. It was time her family saw the woman her godmother trusted to oversee all of this, along with what was close to a million-dollar budget, without thinking she'd disappoint anyone.

"I can't imagine news about me that would be disturbing. What were you told, exactly?"

"I'm sure you know, exactly," was her mother's rather curt response. "You've gotten a bit too friendly with one of the Eddington boys. That's totally inappropriate, Sasha. You're an engaged woman with a reputation to uphold!"

I'm not engaged! Sasha almost bit her tongue to keep the words from spilling out. She knew that now was not the time for that conversation. A phone call with Pamela McDowell already in pit bull mode was not the time or place to break the breakup news.

"You know, Mother, it would have been nice for you to call and ask what happened instead of automatically assuming that what you heard was the truth. Jake's sister Reign invited me to her boyfriend's birthday party. Jake was there. We were having a lively conversation and yes, there may have been a casual touch here or there. Nothing that would warrant calling out the McDowell cavalry as Chrissie's phone call has obviously done."

"He didn't kiss you?"

Sasha was glad to be stopped at a red light as that news gave her pause. She'd determined it impossible for Chrissie to have seen *that* kiss. But she could have seen Jake kiss her hand, or other amorous behavior as they reentered the club's main room.

"Kissing?" Sasha managed a carefree laugh. "We were talking. Laughing. Enjoying the party. Having fun. I don't know why Chrissie felt the need to report that to her cousin, but her interference has blown the situation way out of proportion."

"Whatever happened last night or is happening in

Point du Sable, one thing is being made clear. We need to get you refocused on what matters, your upcoming wedding. It's time you set a date, Sasha, so that the real planning can begin."

"I'll be home next week, Mother. We'll talk then."

Sasha's mom seemed to take her noncommittal reply as consent to move forward with plans she and Ruthanne had made without her inclusion. Her tone softened as she relayed how after the immediate family Thanksgiving meal, the McDowells had been invited to join the Trotters for dessert, drinks and their Christmas tree lighting. She went on about venues and tastings and possible color schemes, oblivious to Sasha's nonparticipation. Sasha arrived at the store for her meeting with the CEO. She bid her mother goodbye, then sat in her car for a couple minutes to take her thoughts from her personal life to Val's pet project. There'd be time to ponder the best way to tell her family about the broken engagement, which for Sasha wasn't the most important conversation. The talk she really needed to have was with Jake. The conversation that would reveal her as the feline he slept with at the party. It was what she'd planned to do last night, followed by the suggestion that they get a room. Running into Chrissie had messed that up. For Sasha it was a mere delay, not a denial. When she returned to Point du Sable after Thanksgiving, she'd be officially single and ready to introduce Zorro to the tigress he'd been looking for.

Ten

Jake finished up a morning meeting, then left the office on his way to the club. He was on edge. He had been that way since Lincoln's cousin, Chrissie, showed up at the party. After running into her, the casual vibe between himself and Sasha never got back on track. She seemed preoccupied, almost nervous. Jake got that, in a way. He and Reign knew that her relationship had ended, but aside from her ex, they were the only ones. His potential business association with Linc aside, the Trotters were an influential DC family. His grandfather was a retired grand bishop of a large congregation and revered everywhere. His mother, Mona, had taught him how society ran. Gossip was the gasoline that fueled their social engines, with high position and stellar pedigrees the vehicle's destinations. It wouldn't be good for scandal to hit. He understood how doing so would be uncomfortable, but why couldn't Sasha just tell them the truth?

That possibility was the second reason he'd gotten little sleep. She said the relationship was over, but was it really? By her own admission there was a long history there, not just with Lincoln but with their families as well. There was love, too, even if it wasn't blinding passion. Was it enough for Sasha to go through with the wedding in order to save face and her family's social standing? Possibly. Love was only one reason women got married. Jake thought about the Eddingtons and their close ties. Controversy was never easy. Having it involve someone close to you was harder. Which was why he couldn't discount the possibility of her changing her mind and getting back with her ex—a thought that hit him like a punch in the gut—specifically because of the third reason he'd lost sleep.

Sasha was the tigress.

Jake hadn't confronted her again but was ninety-eight percent sure he'd uncovered his mystery cat's identity and that her name was Sasha McDowell. The thought had flitted across his mind several times. In each instance he'd dismissed it outright. But last night and the kiss was a game changer. The moment their lips connected and her sweet, soft tongue darted out, demanding entry into a mouth more than willing to let it in, he knew. The way his body reacted, the same as it had at HalloMask. He'd been with scores of women, but Sasha, or whoever had worn the tiger outfit, was the only one who with the merest of touches sent him from zero to sixty in no time flat.

But it couldn't be Sasha. That made no sense. She'd arrived in town that Sunday, the day after the party. During that brunch, she acted nothing like the take-charge woman he'd known mere hours before. Could the unthinkable turn out to be true? It was the best of possibilities and the worst of outcomes. Being true meant he'd slept with his business associate's ex-fiancée. A guy that if their next meeting was as positive as the others had been, could become a part of his team. Sasha being the pussycat would mean that she'd deceived him. And lied. Two traits that Jake abhorred with a passion. Two characteristics he didn't abide at all.

If she wasn't the mystery woman, Jake was still in trouble. No doubt, Sasha felt the attraction as strongly as he did. Clearly, if last night was any indication, she wanted to act on it, as did he. Doing so, however, would create a whole other controversy, and set him and his family at odds with not only the Trotters but the McDowells. Powerful families in the nation's capital, an area that if his business took off could easily become another of Jake's playgrounds. And worse, Sasha's ambassador father was a brother. A member of the uber-powerful, globally influential business fraternity that his own father currently helmed—The Society of Ma'at. He didn't even want to begin to imagine what their secret being uncovered might cause. Sasha's brothers, TJ and Brandon, weren't close friends, but they were valued ones. Linc was a smart guy with experience that would complement what Jake wanted to do. His dad, Elijah Trotter, was also a SOMA member. This was a huge dilemma. Only one person could help him out of it. He checked his watch and engaged his Bluetooth.

"Jake! I was just thinking about you."

Sasha's voice brought out the day's first genuine smile. "All good, I hope."

"If some of it was a little bad, a little naughty, would that be a problem?"

"That might be a big problem."

"A big problem or a thick problem?"

Jake's whole body tensed. "That's some pretty suggestive language, isn't it?"

"You bring out the boldness in me—what can I say?"

A spark of light shot through. "Bold. Like a tiger?"

He gripped the wheel, a mix of anger and excitement building while awaiting her reaction. That she paused increased the mystery-solved percentage from ninety-eight to ninety-nine.

"Yeah, I could say that. Tigers are bold."

"Where are you, Sasha?"

"I'm headed to the country club for lunch with Val and her sorors."

"Perfect, I'm on my way there too."

"I'd invite you to join us but I don't think you'd want to spend an hour talking about fashion, food and toys."

"That's okay. Mine is a business lunch as well. If you can meet me beforehand though, I'd really appreciate it."

"What about afterward? Or tonight? I only have about ten minutes before our meeting starts."

"I'll only need five. There are a series of private rooms adjacent to the main dining area. I'll find out if one is available and text you to meet me there."

"You sound serious, Jake. Any hint of what this is about?"

The tiger reference wasn't enough of one? "It's about us. See you in five."

Jake arrived at the Point du Sable Country Club and headed straight to a door marked Fairway, one of the smaller rooms set up for private affairs. He tapped on the door before opening it to go inside. The room was empty. Sasha hadn't yet arrived. The server had already set a pitcher of lime-and-mint water on the table along with two crystal goblets. Jake bypassed the pristine table setting and walked over to the window. Ominous-looking clouds had replaced last week's sunshine, bringing with them a dip in the temps as well. He hoped the weather wasn't a sign of what was getting ready to happen—his relationship with Sasha going from sunny to stormy.

The door opened. Sasha entered like a whirlwind, a bundle of exquisite energy. Or was it nerves?

"Hey, there! Sorry I didn't get here sooner. This sweet old lady had a fender bender just down the block. I couldn't let her wait for the police by herself." She looked at her watch. "Let me text Val real quick to let her know I'm here but running a couple minutes behind."

The seconds it took her to dash off the text gave Jake a chance to regain his composure. Even in his frustrated state, he appreciated Sasha's appearance. She looked poised and professional in a classic black Chanel dress—a fact he knew because his sister Maeve had a red one—that she wore with glittery black pumps and a strand of onyx pearls. Perfect for lunch with Val and the sorors and nothing like the femme fatale who accosted him on Halloween night.

"Okay. All done." Sasha placed her coat on the rack

and set down a stylish briefcase before walking to where he stood at the window. "Good to see you."

She lifted her arms and stepped forward to give him a hug. In spite of his desire not to, he embraced her and returned it. But only for a second. Any longer and anger would have been replaced by desire, throwing his whole plan out of whack and wasting precious time. This meeting had purpose. Best get to it. He took a step back, placed a hand in a pocket and eyed her intently— something that not only the moment but her beauty seemed to demand.

"Jake, what's the matter? You look upset."

"I have a question—one I want answered truthfully."

"Okay." Answered in that long, drawn-out way that signaled what was happening was not okay at all.

"Did you attend this year's HalloMask party?"

Even before she answered, her expression told him everything he needed to know.

She dropped her eyes. "Yes."

"You're the tiger." She nodded. "We made love."

Slowly, she lifted mesmerizing eyes framed with long, thick lashes. "Yes."

For a few seconds, everything stopped. Time. His thoughts. The world. To believe was one thing, to know, quite another. Sasha was the woman he'd dreamed about, the one he'd determined to locate and invite back into his bed. The truth settled in his groin, arousing and angering him at the same time.

"Why, Sasha? Why did you seduce me like that?"

"It…seemed like a good idea at the time?" she offered, with a half-hearted grin.

"This isn't funny. Official or not, you're still engaged.

Have you forgotten Linc and I are talking about doing major business together? Or that he asked me to keep you away from the wolves? Now, no matter how it's explained he'll think that I am one!"

"I understand why you're angry, Jake. This isn't your fault. It's not completely mine either. When we got together that night, I had no idea it was you. Reign had assured me you wouldn't be there. Said you'd be at the Bears game, that it was one you wouldn't miss. That said, what happened is what I wanted to happen. I've admired you from afar and wondered what you'd be like. I don't regret it. I don't intend on anyone ever finding out but if they do, I'll take full responsibility. I'll say you were tricked. I'll handle Linc and our families. You don't have to get involved."

His eyes scanned her body, then bore into hers. "I'd say it's a bit late for that option."

"I'm sorry. I apologize for what happened. What I did was selfish. I didn't think about you or the consequences, and I should have."

"You should have told me who you were that night, or the next day when I asked you point-blank."

"You're right. Your question caught me off guard. It freaked me out to discover you'd attended the party after all. But at that time, I still didn't know for sure that you were Zorro."

She straightened. Her chin rose slightly, defiantly. "As I said, I apologize for not being honest, Jake, but I'm not sorry that we made love. It was amazing. I want to do it again."

"Dammit, Sasha!" Jake crossed the room to put more distance between them. It was either that or grant her wish by removing her dress and treating her body as his midday meal.

"This is fucked up. I don't even—"

Her ringing phone interrupted. She looked down. "It's Val." She answered. "Val, I'm here. Are you ladies in the main room?…The Grand Slam?…Yes, I know about the hall of private rooms. I'll be right there."

"I've got to go." She reached for her briefcase, gathered her coat and turned. "Is there anything I can say to make this better?"

"No."

"I'm telling everyone about the breakup this weekend. I was going to wait until after Christmas, but they need to know now. When I return to Point du Sable, I'll be officially single. Then maybe we can talk again."

"About what? How you used trickery and lies to put me in this position? How you may have put a very important, very lucrative business opportunity, not to mention my reputation, on the line? No, Sasha. I don't think we'll have anything to talk about."

"Okay."

He barely heard the whisper. Jake watched her leave, then returned to the window. Before, all he'd wanted to do was find his mystery pussycat. Now all he wanted to do was forget he knew her name.

Eleven

Admitting the truth to Jake had been daunting, so much so that after wrapping up Monday's meeting at the club, Sasha packed her bags and flew home two days earlier than originally planned. She was so emotionally drained that when Lincoln insisted on picking her up at the airport, she didn't refuse. They still hadn't talked much. Mostly by text and even then, about impersonal subjects or common acquaintances. TJ was still angry about her hanging up on him and had gone radio silent. Sasha let him stew. She loved her family but it was time for them to see her as she was now instead of the girl they knew ten years ago, before Switzerland, bullying, a brief French romance and finally, sometimes painfully, coming into her own independent self.

When she reached baggage claim, Lincoln was waiting. Seeing him was a clear reminder of what she needed to do—put what had become a farce of a relationship to a clear end. The sooner the better. The hurt on Jake's face and in his voice had moved her. His rejection, though understandable, had stung badly. Only after officially and publicly ending the relationship with Lincoln would she have a chance of working things out with Jake, of him forgiving her and giving them a chance to see if what they had was something real or just a one-night wonder. Sasha preferred the first but would accept the latter. Either way, one thing was clear. She wanted to know.

Lincoln held out his arms as she neared him. "There she is!"

The bear hug surprised her, but they had been friends for more than half of their lives. With that in mind, she hugged him back.

"Hey, Linc."

"It's only been what, barely four weeks since I've seen you? If feels like forever. You look great!"

"Thanks."

"Uh-oh. What's that tone I hear in your voice? Is everything okay?"

It was all Sasha could do to not look at him as though he'd grown three heads. No, everything was not okay. Had he forgotten that life had shifted and they'd broken up? Or maybe this was Lincoln postbreakup, already healed and ready to move on.

"I guess I'm just tired. It's been a busy past few weeks. Deciding to come home now made today a rush. But I'm here!"

"Yeah, I was surprised when your mom called saying you'd changed your plans. She was equally curious to find out you hadn't told me."

"Lincoln…"

"I know. We're on a break." He gave her a devilish look. "But that's our little secret."

Sasha couldn't pin down the feeling, but Lincoln's behavior was strange. Since baggage claim wasn't the best place for serious discussions, she let him lead with small talk until they'd retrieved her luggage and loaded up the car. Once they were on I-395 heading toward her condo, she felt ready to share her heart.

"Linc, I think we need to make the announcement."

"About breaking up?" he said as lightly as asking to pass the Grey Poupon. "I don't think so."

"I know it's Thanksgiving. But Mom told me about our families getting together after dinner. We can tell everyone at the same time."

"How long are we going to do this for this time, Sasha? Last time lasted what, two months? Or that other time when we took a break for the summer right after senior year? Usually, it's the guy who gets cold feet but I know women can too. It's why I've been so patient. But now it's time for us to grow up."

That Lincoln wasn't taking the breakup seriously had crossed her mind. Now the niggling fear had been confirmed. Even more of a reason not to keep their status a secret past Thursday night.

"Is that what you think this is about? Me not being mature enough to know what I want?"

"That's not what I said."

"It's what you implied. I'm not a little girl anymore, Linc. That's the reason why this time I won't change my mind. Those other times, I went against my better judgment and stayed together. But I did it for you, TJ, Mom and Dad. I did it for your parents and what everyone expected. This time, the decision is for me."

Lincoln remained quiet. She looked over to see him surprisingly calm, could have even sworn there was a bit of a smirk on his face. Was it because he and Jake might become business partners? Did he think she'd stay with him for optical purposes, on the basis of good PR?

"You know I'll always care for you, right? That the love I have for you will never go away. But the feelings I have for you are like those for a good friend, a wonderful friend, but not a husband. It was wrong of me to keep being your girlfriend when my heart wasn't truly there."

"Grand and Pop are here."

There it was. The secret weapon.

"Your grandparents are back in DC? After moving to Barbados, they swore to never see another winter in the northeast."

Lincoln smiled openly as he looked at her. "Our upcoming nuptials have Pop all excited. He hasn't even considered someone else officiating. They've planned a grand lunch for us this Sunday at Fogo de Chão."

Around DC, Lincoln's grandfather the Esteemed Bishop Dr. Archibald Trotter was legendary. He'd been a spiritual advisor to presidents, a voice of reason in civil and political crises, and quite possibly had officiated more marriages and baptisms than all other area ministers combined. In short, he was revered throughout the district, and other cities as well.

"You bastard."

"What? I didn't send the invitation."

"It was undoubtedly from your mother, and I'm sure you knew all about it."

"Come on, Sasha. Why do you want to break up with me? Is it because you're afraid? Is it Jake? He's a great businessman. I'm actually looking forward to working with the guy. But if you're considering him for personal reasons, there are some things you should know about how he treats women."

"And how's that?"

"Like they're a dime a dozen."

"And you know this how?"

"I have my ways of finding these things out."

"How long are your grandparents going to be here?"

"Less than a week. We'll see them again soon, when the family spends Christmas in Barbados. I know you love the island. We'll have a fantastic time."

Sasha sighed. So far nothing about her return home was going according to plan. "I'd like to speak with them before they leave. For marital counseling. To find out if they think it wise for me to marry someone I care about but am not in love with."

The comment made Lincoln less cocky, but he'd planted the seed. Breaking up in front of their parents and siblings was bad enough. For his grandparents to witness the breakup would be excruciating. They'd been married fifty-plus years, an institution held sacred, which would hopefully work in Sasha's favor if she engaged them in an honest conversation. Could she get up the nerve to do it? And at what cost?

Thanksgiving Day came and went without an announcement. Sasha simply couldn't bring herself to disrupt the tree trimming festivities at the Trotters that everyone so enjoyed. All except her. The entire night, her stomach roiled. At Lincoln's request and to avoid questions, she put on the two-carat engagement ring that she hadn't worn in more than a month. Lincoln, TJ and her other brother, Brandon, were almost inseparable, cracking jokes and competing at every chance. Chrissie acted as though the party run-in never happened and no rumors were spread. The one bright spot was Lincoln's grandparents. Sasha thoroughly enjoyed them. She even got along with Millie, Lincoln's much older, ultraconservative sister whom she barely knew. The evening served up one minor win. When the grandparents offered their congratulations, she asked Cora, affectionately called Grand, if they could have a private conversation before Sunday's dinner. Cora graciously agreed. Sasha would tell the wise older woman the truth about her situation. Grand Cora would know what to do.

Having made that decision, Sasha felt lighter. So much so that when Lincoln said he had tickets for all of them to attend a Wizards game, she was actually excited. On Friday she and Lincoln, along with her brothers and their dates, scooted their way to excellent seats near the floor of the Capital One Arena. Lincoln patiently pointed out players and positions. The group had fun spotting celebrities in the crowd. Mostly, Sasha thought about how much more fun the night would be if she were there with Jake instead of those around her. They hadn't spoken since their tense exchange that day at the club. She figured next week, once she'd given Lincoln his ring back, would be soon enough to start making peace offerings. Her luck might be better if they talked face-to-face.

A nudge from Lincoln brought her out of her musings.

"Look! We're on camera."

Sasha looked up to see their faces beaming from a KissCam, the sound of the crowd's encouragement rolling in like a fog. Before she could think, let alone react, Lincoln gave her a big smooch, then reached for her hand and held it up to the camera. The lights from the arena made the diamond sparkles dance. The crowd roared their appreciation, assuming they'd just gotten engaged. Sasha covered her embarrassment and anger behind a smile but as soon as the camera moved to the next unsuspecting pair, she stood and made an announcement.

"I'm leaving."

And that's exactly what she did.

Twelve

Sasha's revelation made focusing almost impossible. Jake tried to pull it off, but very little could be put past a group who'd known him his entire life. The business luncheon consisted of his father, Derrick, his brother, Desmond, and his brother-from-another-mother Cayden Barker. The latter took the first lapse in conversation to shine the spotlight on Jake's mood.

"What's up, man? You're looking like someone stole your puppy."

Jake gave a lopsided smile to try and deflect. "It's nothing, Cayden. A bit tired is all."

Desmond reached for his water. "Tired of what? I've been watching the companies we favor for investments. Your client's portfolios must be rising through the roof."

"True."

"The players must be happy. So work can't be it."

"Didn't I read a business plan involving you and TJ McDowell?" Derrick asked.

"Me and TJ's good friend Linc Trotter," Jake corrected.

"Business plan?" Cayden gave Jake a playful punch. "Holding out on your brothers, I see."

"Just hadn't gotten around to sharing what is still in the embryo stage."

"What's the business?" Desmond asked.

"An independent financial consulting service. I handle the guys' investments, but many of them have more general questions regarding finances—budgeting, real estate, cryptocurrency, trusts and wills, setting up estates. I'm thinking of putting together a company with a team of experts in all areas, but centered around pro sports, to put on seminars specifically for these highly paid athletes and then of course have Eddington Enterprise be the one-stop shop for all those financial and business needs."

"How does Lincoln fit in?"

"When there's this level of money being discussed politics are always involved, especially when it comes to legislation that would favor their bank accounts. Linc would be an excellent liaison, someone to help me navigate Washington's shark-infested waters."

Desmond's expression was thoughtful. "I didn't know you and Linc were that well acquainted."

"We've traveled in the same circles for years. A few months ago, I ran into TJ. He asked me what I was into and I casually mentioned my idea. TJ's expertise is in company creation and buyouts, bankruptcy reorganizations and nonprofits. I thought he might be interested in joining me. His plate is full. He mentioned Linc. We've only talked a couple times. Real progress won't begin until after the first of the year."

"Is that why you've been on hiatus?" Cayden eyed his best friend as he took a drink. "Word has it you've been fairly quiet on the social scene."

"Whoever gave you that word is misinformed."

"Were they also wrong about your feelings for Sasha?"

Jake caught the scowl before it hit his face and leaned against his chair. "Sounds like Reign has been sharing her speculations with your wife. Tell Avery she knows nothing."

"Sasha as in Linc's fiancée?" Derrick asked. "They are still engaged, aren't they?"

Jake felt three pairs of eyes on him before answering, "As far as I know."

"Too bad," Cayden said, finishing a last bite of seafood before pushing back his plate. "Sasha's a beautiful woman. Smart too." He turned toward Desmond. "Did you know my wife is trying to recruit her to work at On Point?"

"How'd that work with her living in DC?"

"If Avery had her way, she'd relocate here."

"Linc is a Trotter." Derrick gave a quick head shake. "He'd never leave the capitol."

"Would you move to DC, Jake?" Cayden asked.

"I might end up buying a place somewhere in the area but my roots are in Point du Sable."

Jake returned to work and put in several hours before having dinner and enjoying a Bulls game from one of the owner's suites. It was late when he returned to the estate. He didn't care. He had some questions to ask his sister. He reminded himself that he was angry with Sasha, had no investment in her future, no intention of seeing her when she returned to PDS. Still, something wouldn't let him totally dismiss her. At least from his mind. No one else had to know about that right?

Instead of parking near his spread on the north wing, he pulled up to the side where his sister resided. If Reign wasn't up, she would be, shortly. He entered her domain and walked directly to her suite.

Passing through the marble columns that marked the entrance he called out, "Reign! Are you up?"

Within seconds, a pajamas-clad Reign emerged from her room. "I am now," she said, yawning and squinting at the clock. It was after midnight. "Why are you waking me up?" She plopped on the couch and put her bare feet on a coffee table. "Missing Sasha?"

Jake sat down in a nearby chair. "I don't know what you're talking about, but obviously you've been talking."

"Only to family. Didn't she go home for Thanksgiving?"

"I guess."

"Then you totally know. I don't blame you, brother. She's way more beautiful than I remembered. She's also TJ's sister. And—" she used air quotes "—engaged."

"I know all that. What you got to drink in here?"

"Everything."

He stood. "You want something?"

Reign shook her head. He left and soon returned with a bottle of beer, determined to detour the subject from the very reason he'd come to her suite. "Hey, we never talked about your trip to LA. How was it?"

"Warm. Crowded. Ace and London's fashion show was a hit, as always."

Jake nodded.

Reign's look was one of mischief. "So…you came over here at midnight to talk about clothes?"

"Outside of business, what do you know about her fiancé?"

"You mean her husband, Ace?"

"Not London, Sasha."

"The one you had no idea I was talking about?" She laughed. "Not much."

"She told me the two of you had lunch."

"We did. This may come as breaking news, but women talk about more than men. He has an older sister," she continued when Jake remained silent. "His dad works in politics."

Jake knew about Elijah Trotter. His son was the enigma.

"I'm not talking about information that's public knowledge. I'm talking about Linc's personal life."

Reign chuckled. "I know. Their families seem to be longtime friends but honestly, she didn't talk about him much."

"What did the two of you talk about?"

Reign shrugged. "My trip. The Point. You."

"What about me?" he casually asked.

"Where you went to school, if you were dating, stuff like that."

"What did you tell her?"

"The truth. You're a whore."

Jake almost spewed his drink. "Sis!"

Reign laughed out loud. "Just kidding, brother. I'd never reveal your secrets."

"I am not a whore."

"No, you're not. You just like variety."

"I'm a healthy, single man. What's wrong with that?"

"Nothing."

"My tastes are very discriminating."

"Who are you trying to convince?" Reign yawned. "Looks like the two of you had a good time at the party."

"You saw us together?"

"Briefly. At one point I was heading over to speak with you when someone else came up. I got sidetracked and didn't see her again."

"Sasha didn't stay too much longer after that." Jake pondered how much he should tell his sister and decided to stick close with what she already knew. "The woman that came up to us is Linc's cousin."

"That's no big deal. Is it?"

"Could be. Sasha and I were fooling around. Lightweight, nothing serious. Except the cousin may have seen us."

"She's no longer engaged. You don't know?"

"It's not official. I know. The families don't."

"Oh." Said with much more understanding than seconds before.

"They're supposed to announce the breakup this week."

"Happy Thanksgiving."

"Yeah. Right."

Reign stood. "I'm flying out early mañana to attend Trenton's game, and need sleep." She headed toward the hallway, stopped just before turning the corner. "I haven't seen you this interested in a woman in a long time. For the record, I like Sasha. She likes you. I don't know why you're fighting it."

"She lied to me."

"About what?"

"That's her story to tell."

"Why'd she do it?"

"Lie? I don't know."

"Maybe you should ask her. Night, Jake."

Thanksgiving was filled with fun and family. Reign's words stayed on Jake's mind. So did Sasha. More than once, he started to call her, especially later the night she was supposed to break the news to her family. Not getting a call or text from her made him change his mind. If she went through with her plans and made the breakup official, he'd then begin to think about searching out more details on why she'd continued to deceive him after the party, once she'd figured out the identity of the man behind the mask. Based on her answer, he might be open to seeing where life could lead them. She never called but by Friday night, he could admit that he was looking forward to her returning to Point. He was ready to take Reign's advice and at least hear her out. From what his mother told him from talking with Val, that would be Monday, just days away. When Cayden called with a game night invite, Jake was ready for fun.

He reached the block of his destination and took in the corner building with a critical eye. It was a popular sports bar named Third & Long. He pulled up to the valet stand, noted the cars that lined the block and the boisterous-looking crowd that could be seen from a line of huge square windows. Inside, he instantly noted a few familiar faces along with a wink or wave from more than one appreciative female. He nodded a cordial response but kept moving toward his destination, the VIP section on the second floor.

"Jake! What's up, man?" The bouncer held up a bear claw otherwise known as a hand for a fist pump and leaned over for a one-shoulder tap. "Cayden hasn't been too long getting here." He nodded toward a booth behind them.

Jake spotted Cayden along with several familiar faces. He turned back to the bouncer. "Good seeing you."

"Always. If you need anything, let me know."

After stopping to chat with a client who played pro baseball and another athlete hugged up with a popular Instagram model, Jake reached the booth and slid inside.

"About time you got here," was Cayden's greeting.

"Busy man, what can I say?"

"No worries."

"It's been a while since I've been here," Jake said looking around. "I like what they've done to the place."

The bank of televisions across the bar, not to mention the picture being projected against the entire back wall, gave everyone on both floors a front row seat to the action of multiple games across several states. Most of the screens were on the local basketball team's matchup against a big rival, but a few were tuned to other games in the league. His eyes swept the room, admiring the sophisticated decor that featured stone walls, mahogany floors, stainless steel tables for four and semiprivate booths covered in brushed kid leather.

"Are you seeing what I'm seeing?"

"Buying the business?"

Cayden nodded. "Taking it private. Upgrading to a full-service restaurant and transforming the third floor, now basically used for storage, into the VIP lounge. We could make the Jake and Bake magic happen again."

They both laughed at the high school nickname they'd been given. Cayden leaned forward, his grayish-green eyes sparkling with enthusiasm. "What could be a more perfect fit for the person who handles many of the top player's finances than to add a sports bar to the equation?"

"That may be the problem. Keeping a professional distance from these guys is how I maintain the edge."

"I get that." Cayden thoughtfully rubbed his five-o'clock shadow. "You could be a silent partner."

Jake nodded. "That's a possibility." His phone rang. He looked at Cayden. "Here's another one, potentially."

"One what?"

"Problem. Linc Trotter."

Cayden's brow rose.

Jake answered the phone. "Jake Eddington." He pulled an earbud from his pocket and put it on to hear better. "Not really. Hanging out. Knocking back a few beers…Oh, really?…Yes, it's detailed. I wanted it that way. What'd you think?"

Jake gave Cayden a thumbs-up. "Glad to hear that, Linc. And glad you called me. I didn't want that little dustup about Sasha to get in the way of business…Hey, man, no worries. I would have behaved the same way. I totally understand…No, next week is perfect. Great, we'll talk then."

Jake ended the call, feeling uneasy. That it was the day after Thanksgiving and Lincoln still sounded very much like a man engaged gave Jake pause. Clearly, Sasha hadn't made the breakup official. What his potential business partner didn't know increased his discomfort—the accidental Halloween tryst. His growing feelings for someone off-limits.

"Linc read the proposal. He thinks it's solid. Wants to talk next week about how the company might be structured. He has several high-end contacts as potential investors."

"Working that close to Sasha isn't going to be a problem?"

"Not for me."

"But she's the potential of a problem you mentioned before answering the phone."

Jake nodded, remembering that Cayden didn't know about the secret breakup, or what had happened between him and Sasha. He decided to keep it that way until next week, when Sasha returned and she was officially single. If that was even the case. Given Lincoln's upbeat tone, Jake wasn't sure.

The guys ordered dinner, then socialized with several mutual friends. A second round of games began. His vision settled on a TV screen beyond Cayden. Jake saw that the Wizards were playing tonight. Seeing the Washington, DC, team made him immediately think of Sasha and wonder how she was. What she was doing. He imagined her dropping her bombshell news sometime that weekend, and the fallout from disappointing her parents. Who would help her get through it? He wished it were him. He almost called TJ but thought better of it. Knowing how much TJ loved basketball, Jake figured he might be at the game. He shifted over to the screen on the wall, the one showing another of his favorite teams. Halftime was approaching on several networks. Jake considered leaving and watching the rest of the games at home.

"Look at the lovebirds."

He turned to see what had caused the sarcasm and slight shock in Cayden's voice.

Cayden leaned forward, his voice low as he asked, "Isn't that Sasha?"

Jake viewed the screen he'd just turned away from. It was indeed Sasha on the KissCam with Lincoln beside her. Kissing her. Before he could process that bit of information, there was more to take in. Lincoln held up Sasha's hand, one very much sporting a ring. The one she never wore while in Point du Sable. The crowd went wild. Jake became numb. It appeared that Sasha and Linc were still very much engaged. For whatever reason, she'd lied again. Sasha wouldn't return to PDS a single woman. The reason she'd changed her mind didn't matter. Only the facts, which were now clear.

Jake felt like a fool. It was time to move past that night with Sasha. It was time for him to forget the tigress. Bury the secret that existed between them. Put that night behind him. Everything happened in divine order, the girlfriend of one of his clients once told him. In possibly getting ready to work with Linc, being clear about the status of his engagement had been necessary. Knowing that Sasha lacked integrity was crucial. Knowing the truth was for the best.

Thirteen

They'd been in the car twenty minutes and still Sasha hadn't spoken to Lincoln, who'd followed her out of the arena, down the VIP tunnel and into the parking lot. With paparazzi nipping at their heels, Sasha had conceded when he'd led them to his limo and eased her inside. But now, in the private confines of the shiny black car, Sasha could finally react to Lincoln's audacity, what he'd taken public against her wishes, and in a way, forced her hand.

Or so he thought.

Lincoln's actions had shocked her into clarity. They had solidified for Sasha what until now hadn't been definitively acknowledged. In breaking the engagement, she'd absolutely, unequivocally made the right decision. There was no going back. When it came to her and Lincoln being a couple, Sasha was done. She hated to disappoint Lincoln's grandparents, along with their families and God knew who else, but Sasha would not continue being dishonest. With Jake, she'd learned again what she already knew—lying didn't pay. The feeling of incredulity followed by shock, then hurt, then anger that had hit her in the middle of the arena, with the spotlight beaming and her stunned face plastered on the KissCam, had morphed into one of steely resolve. Her desire to live a life she chose with the person she desired outweighed any fear from however the chips might fall because of her decisions. She felt the tightness of tension in her shoulders and relaxed them. Her sigh was audible.

She glanced over at Lincoln's expression, unreadable as he gazed out the window. "I can't believe you did that."

"It wasn't planned." When he turned to face her, his look was sincere.

"I can actually believe that part." Sasha's eyes drifted from his to look straight ahead. Looking at Lincoln made her angry. Being mad was not productive at a moment like this.

"I also know that once you saw us on the screen, with millions watching, you made a conscious decision to make even more public a relationship you know is over. Just like you orchestrated your grandparents' visit. To try and force me to remain somewhere I don't want to be."

"What do you expect me to do? Let you ride off into the sunset with the man who betrayed the trust of me and your family?"

"Jake didn't betray anyone."

"But you don't deny that you're seeing him."

"This has nothing to do with Jake." She took a breath before turning to look Lincoln in the eye. "No, Jake and I are not seeing each other. However, I won't deny that there is an attraction."

"Was Chrissie right, that the two of you were together at that party?"

"We were both there and ran into each other. I was having fun, teasing and flirting."

Another pause and then, "I kissed him."

"Just like Chrissie said! That's probably not all you did."

Sasha was not going to tell Lincoln about what happened at the other party.

"Even though we'd secretly ended things, I shouldn't have done it. Don't get angry at Jake for what happened. It was my fault. Something I initiated. This news has to hurt and I'm sorry. I wish things could have ended differently."

Sasha began to remove the engagement ring.

"Don't."

"Linc, this is over. It's time you accept it. I shouldn't have given in to your pleas. I shouldn't have perpetuated a lie this weekend by wearing this ring."

"What about Sunday's dinner? Grand and Pop are so excited. Everyone will be there."

"And everyone will know my decision. It will be very difficult for me, Lincoln. But it has to be done."

She eased the baguette cut off her finger.

Lincoln turned toward the window. "For God's sake, don't do that. I'm not taking it back."

"I can't keep it."

"I don't want it," he repeated through gritted teeth.

The remainder of the ride was silent torture. When they reached Sasha's condo, she was not surprised to feel tears.

"Linc..." Words caught in her throat.

"Look, Sasha, save it, okay. We've been through this before. I believe you really mean it this time. So just go."

"We were friends first, Lincoln. I hope that someday, when we've healed from the breakup, we can be friends again."

Silence.

"I'll always care about you. I know this hurts. I'm sorry."

"Driver, show Ms. McDowell to her door."

Sasha made sure Lincoln saw her place the ring on the seat, then eased out of the car. A wave of sadness washed over her. She let the tears fall. Part of the anguish was due to what happened tonight. Part was in anticipation of what would happen next.

The fallout was worse than expected. Dinner was a disaster. It was all Sasha's fault. The day started out well enough—perfect actually—much like the day before. That Saturday she'd made up with TJ and spent enjoyable quality time with her family. Lincoln seemed to have finally come to terms with her decision, so much so that she changed her mind about meeting with Grand. It was no longer necessary to receive marital advice. Still, Lincoln demanded she wait until the end of dinner to make the announcement. She reluctantly agreed. Almost immediately upon arrival, however, she knew that waiting was a bad idea.

"There's the bride-to-be!" Pop exclaimed, his arms outstretched. "What a welcomed addition you will be to our family."

"And such a pretty one too." Grand beamed. "Have you considered a destination wedding? If so, Barbados is beautiful all year round."

During appetizers, Sasha endured an extensive conversation with her mom and Ruthanne involving dates, colors and what numbers were appropriate for the wedding party and guest list. Ruthanne thought that around three hundred was adequate. Because of her husband's position and internationally-wide political circle, Sasha's mom thought five hundred more appropriate. Every time Sasha looked over at Lincoln he was smiling, his posture one of satisfaction, like a chess player who'd made all the right moves. Even the staid Mr. Trotter loosened up enough for an extended conversation involving the importance of her position as a future society wife.

When he suggested she take her cues from her mother, Pamela, and Ruthanne, two stellar examples of good partners, he'd added, something in Sasha snapped. Somewhere between the busboys removing salad plates and hearing the strains of a Boyz II Men love song reprised as a classical tune, she found herself standing with a water goblet in one hand, and a fork in the other, quickly clanging them together until all eyes were on her.

"I need to make an announcement," she blurted, swallowing a well of emotion that sprang up unexpectedly. She swiped away unwelcomed tears and gripped the table for support. "There's something I have to share with all of you. Something we," she looked at Lincoln, who refused to meet her eye, "something that I should have told all of you long before now. But we've all been having such a good time, and Grand and Pop are here, and it just…"

Sasha took a sip of water, kept her eyes away from the chagrined look on her mother's face, and took another sip to gather herself. *You can do this.*

"Almost two months ago, Lincoln and I broke up. There will be no wedding."

She mentally braced herself against the expected gasps and surprised outbursts, quickly glanced away from her ambassador father's stunned expression, her mother's and Ruthanne's horrified ones, and political afficionado Trotter's look of disdain.

"Darling, what happened?" Grand asked, genuinely perplexed and more importantly for Sasha, obviously concerned. "Was this why you wanted to speak with me?"

The compassion that oozed from the older woman's voice was like steel for Sasha's spine. Back straightened, shoulders squared, she looked at Cora and spoke clearly.

"Yes, Grand. I wanted your wisdom. Lincoln and I secretly ended our engagement in September, but he was hoping I'd change my mind. I know how much our wedding meant to both families and agreed to delay the announcement. But no more. I've made my decision."

"Sasha!" Her mom's cultured voice had not risen but cut through the room. "Sit down. This is neither the time nor the place to discuss such personal matters." She looked at TJ. "Son, could you please pass the basket of rolls," her tone even and warm. "I tried the ones seasoned with rosemary and thyme. They're incredible."

TJ quietly reached for the basket and passed it to his left. Ruthanne took a sip of water. Mr. Trotter cleared his throat before taking out a handkerchief and wiping a sweat-free brow.

Thomas, Senior broke the silence. "You heard your mother, Sasha. You will handle this matter with your fiancé privately."

"No, Father," Sasha replied, her voice strong despite the tremor of nerves coursing through her body. "What I have to say cannot wait."

"We're all family here," the elder Bishop Trotter intoned, his voice rich and authoritative. "This is obviously difficult for your daughter. I say we let the young lady speak."

Sasha could have run over and kissed the old man. "Thank you, Pop—excuse me, Bishop Trotter. This is very hard, and not at all the dinner conversation you were expecting. I sincerely apologize for the embarrassment caused. I have so much respect for everyone in this room and would do almost anything not to disappoint you. That is why I can't allow this afternoon to continue without everyone knowing the truth. I broke up with Lincoln just before my godmother, Val Baldwin, asked me to visit Point du Sable and assist with her annual children's benefit. Linc asked that I wait until after the holidays to make the announcement. He hoped whatever was wrong could be fixed, worked out. But it can't."

She looked at Lincoln, who still refused to meet her eye. "This isn't because of anything Linc did. It's me. I don't have the type of feelings for him that I should have if we were to marry. We've known each other practically all of our lives and are better being friends than lifelong partners. I'm sorry, everybody."

"What do you have to say about this, son?" Mr. Trotter asked.

"What can I say?" Lincoln's voice was that of anger mixed with hurt. "She's made her decision. Guess that's the end of it."

The room was eerily quiet. Finally, Bishop Trotter spoke again. "No matter our opinions, Miss Sasha has articulated the matter quite clearly. I for one, however, believe that a person should never let a bit of bad news get in the way of a good steak. Let's continue to enjoy the dinner, and one another, and I'll counsel with the couple later tonight."

It was a good thought, but after Sasha's announcement there was very little enjoyment and for Sasha, aside from Grand, no one who seemed to empathize with or even understand her position. She felt shunned, while on the other side of the room quiet conversations were happening with Lincoln, accompanied by looks of sympathy for him coupled with glares of contempt shot her way. Once dinner was over, she thanked Grand and Pop for coming, politely declined the minister's counsel and walked over to her mother who was standing alone, looking at but probably not seeing a painting on the wall.

"How dare you," Pamela hissed, without looking over. "I have never been so humiliated in my entire life."

"Mother, I—"

With the utmost composure, Pamela cut off Sasha's comment with a quick, barely perceptible move of her hand. She even managed to curve her lips upward, though there was no joy in her eyes.

"We will talk later. You will fix this. We've held the

engagement party. The news is out. I will not have your immature thinking and selfish actions bring a stain on the family name and become gossip mill fodder.

"Time will ease today's discomfort. We'll act as though that undisciplined outburst of yours never occurred. You have until Val's benefit to get yourself together. When you return, we'll announce a date for the wedding."

Sasha inhaled a fortifying breath. "Lincoln and I are not getting married."

Pamela took a step toward Sasha and lowered her voice even more. "Then your father and I will cut you off financially. We'll repossess the condo, end the lease on your car. Defy me and there will be stiff consequences. If you choose to go down this unfortunate road, don't bother coming home once the benefit in Chicago is over."

Fourteen

Monday morning, Jake was awakened by his buzzing cell phone. He hoped it was from Sasha. It was Lincoln.

"Seven o'clock in the morning, man," he answered amid a yawn. "This had better be good."

Instead of a cheeky retort, there was silence.

Jake sat up against the headboard. "Hello?"

"You've got a hell of a lot of nerve."

"Excuse me? What's this about?"

"You know exactly what this is about."

"No," Jake replied, easing out of bed and slipping into a robe. "Actually, I don't."

But he did.

"Was it always your plan to try and steal Sasha away from me? Is that why you reached out to me to start a consulting business? So that you'd have a legitimate excuse to be near my soon-to-be wife?"

Jake reached the kitchen, popped a cup of dark roast into the machine and hit the button. Clearly, this convo would require coffee, something stronger if it weren't so early in the day.

"Linc, after seeing you and Sasha on TV the other night, this is the last type of call from you I expected."

"Sasha told me everything."

Jake's body tensed. Poker time. He forced a light-weight casualness into his voice. "Considering what I saw happen at the Wizards game, couldn't have been too much."

"Are you going to deny that you've been spending time with her? Messing around? Getting physical?"

"You knew Sasha and I had spent time together. I never hid that from you. It's basically what you'd asked me to do."

"Don't you dare take a request of a man I thought upright and ethical, a brother I planned to do business with, and try and make your inappropriate behavior somehow my fault."

"That's not what I'm doing. Something else I'm not going to do is argue with you about what you think happened between me and Sasha, or what someone said happened or whatever you heard that has you this hyped before eight a.m."

"I can't believe I trusted you, was actually excited about partnering up to do business together."

"It probably wouldn't be too presumptive of me to say that deal is off."

"You cocky motherf—"

"Let's keep our mothers out of this." Jake took a sip of steaming hot coffee.

"You're over there all calm and smug. I can ruin you. You have no idea the enemy you've made."

"You should know that I don't scare easily nor take threats well. Do or say anything that tarnishes the Eddington name, and you'll be in a whole heap of trouble. I promise you that."

Jake ended the call. Now angry at both Lincoln and Sasha, he quelled the desire to throw the mug of coffee against the wall and instead walked to his bedroom, changed into sweats and headed over to the main wing's fully equipped gym.

Ninety minutes later he felt calmer, looked like a boss and was ready to begin his workday. While working out, he'd received a text from his assistant that his first appointment had canceled. He started out the door with the thought to grab breakfast at a new restaurant getting rave reviews, then changed his mind and went in search of his mother. She was often in the solarium around this time. Maybe they could have breakfast together and if the opportunity presented itself, maybe he could share enough of what had happened with Sasha to get her perspective.

Jake was right. Mona was in the solarium. But she wasn't alone. Val was with her and didn't look happy.

"Good morning, ladies!"

Mona looked up and smiled. "Hello, son. This is a surprise. To what do I owe this rare pleasure?"

"Client canceled," he said, reaching for a stem of grapes from the fruit bowl as he walked around to greet Val. "Thought I'd have breakfast with my favorite lady."

He squeezed Val's shoulders. "Hello, Mrs. Baldwin."

"Hello, Jake." She smiled, but her eyes held sadness.

He took one of the empty chairs. The conversation he'd seen in progress when walking up to the table was now on hold.

"I'm sorry. Did I interrupt a private conversation?" He half stood. "If that's the case, I can leave."

He watched Mona glance at Val, who slowly shook her head. "No, Jake. It's fine. I was sharing news with your mother that you'll soon hear anyway. Sasha ended her engagement to Lincoln."

"Oh." That her comment surprised him was an understatement. Even with the conversation he'd had with Linc just hours before, it was the last thing he'd expected to hear. He kept his face neutral and hoped for a tone to match. "Wow."

"Her family is extremely upset. Over-the-top if you ask me. Her mother, Pamela, all but threatened to disown her."

"You're kidding." Mona's frown conveyed her annoyance.

"I wish I were. Poor girl is only trying to follow her heart. They should be glad she had the courage to tell that man the truth rather than go through with a ceremony for appearances. Neither family sees it that way, and that's a shame. Lincoln isn't being supportive either and that doesn't help."

Jake's mind was awhirl with questions, ones mostly only Sasha could answer. "Is Sasha still helping with your event?"

Val nodded. "Thank goodness she has that to distract her. When I went to bed last night around midnight, she was still up working."

"She's back already?"

"I picked her up at the airport last night. She was supposed to be back today but the row with her family was so intense she thought it best to put distance between them."

The family chef came over. "Good morning, Mr. Eddington. What can I get you this morning?"

"Nothing for me, John. I'm on my way out."

"I thought you were going to join us for breakfast," Mona said.

He stood and kissed his mom on the cheek. "I just remembered something that I need to do."

On his way to the car, Jake pulled out his phone and dialed Sasha. The anger he'd felt at the sports bar and earlier this morning had been replaced by something else—concern.

"Sasha, it's me. Jake."

"Hi." Her voice was low and raspy.

"Have you been crying?"

Pause. "No."

Her voice told Jake otherwise. "Val's here having breakfast with Mom. I heard what happened."

"You probably think I deserve it."

"Where are you? We need to talk."

"I don't need your pity, Jake."

"Are you at Val's?"

"Yes," she whispered.

"Stay there. I'm on my way."

Moments later, he reached the quiet cul-de-sac and tried the door handle. It was unlocked. He entered.

"Sasha?"

A long pause was followed by, "In here."

He walked toward the sound and found a disheveled beauty on the couch, a throw around her shoulder, her legs tucked beneath her. He went over, sat down and pulled her into his arms. For several moments they stayed that way, Sasha's silent tears wetting his designer suit.

"My family's not speaking to me," she finally managed, her voice strained with the remaining unshed tears.

"They're angry."

Sasha shook her head as she pushed away from his chest. "It's more than that." She reached over for a tissue and blew her nose. "I've done the absolute worst thing you can do in my parents' eyes. I've brought embarrassment to their doorstep. They're ashamed of me."

"Because you broke up with a man you're no longer in love with? That's ridiculous."

"It is, but that's how they feel. For Mother and Father, it's all about decorum. I've broken a societal code."

Sasha eased off the couch and moved to a nearby chair. She reached for another tissue, before wiping her nose and then dabbing her eyes. Her voice grew stronger as she stood and walked to a window.

"All my life, I've done what I was told. I behaved as expected. I followed all the rules. I tried my best to be the daughter they wanted and for the most part, I succeeded in portraying that image.

"It was the same with my brothers. From the time I was born, they were instilled with the belief that I was one to be looked after, protected and to an extent, told what to do. I love TJ and Brandon. They're only doing what they were taught by a structured military man turned US ambassador who was long on discipline but short on outward affection. Both of them, but especially TJ, inherited that same uncompromising nature. Growing up I did what subordinates do. I fell in line and pretended to be okay with it. But there was a cost."

"What was that?" Jake softly asked.

Sasha returned to the chair and sat. "Me."

Sasha went on to tell Jake about her years at boarding school, how difficult it was in those first, early years—the loneliness, pressure and feelings of being isolated from all that was familiar. She was picked on and bullied by jealous classmates. It was new territory for a girl who'd been the apple of her family's eye.

"What happened when you told your parents about it?"

"I only told Mother and then, only so much. Dad didn't bother with such things."

"What did your mom say?"

A bittersweet smile appeared on Sasha's face. "Basically, to suck it up and not do anything to bring embarrassment to the family. Don't make the school have to call her about something negative. Me and my brothers were constantly reminded of our dad's high-profile position. What we did was a reflection on how well he led his family, which in turn, in Mom's eyes, impacted how others viewed his leadership abilities overall. Her response to whatever problem or situation I brought to her was never about me. It was always about protecting Dad's reputation, her social standing and the family name."

For a moment, Jake felt too angry to respond. To put so much expectation on a child was inexcusable.

"I don't mean to disrespect your mom," he finally

responded, "but I've got to say this. What she told you was bullshit. Your feelings mattered. What happened to you mattered and shouldn't have been ignored. You are more important than anything in politics or society. Just in case nobody ever told you that, now you know."

Sasha offered a wisp of a smile. "Thanks, Jake. I don't know that I believe all of what you said, but it's good to hear."

"I have something else to tell you that won't be so pleasant."

"Oh, no," she groaned. "I don't know if I can handle anything else right now."

"Yes, but you need to know. Linc called me."

"He did? When?"

"This morning." Jake gave her an abbreviated version of the conversation. He told her how angry Lincoln was about what happened. He left out the parting threats.

"Despite what either you or I say, he believes I'm responsible for the breakup. He said you told him everything. Did you?"

"Only about that night at Trenton's party, not...the other one."

"He doesn't know we slept together?"

"No, and even if he did, he also knows that he and I had broken up before I came here. Before you were even in the picture. He's just lashing out."

Jake ran a frustrated hand over his freshly shaved face. How had he gotten in the middle of this messy breakup? And why did it have to happen now, when he was on the verge of starting a business and would be doing major networking over the next six months? He wasn't afraid of Lincoln's threats, but disparaging talk about him could cause unnecessary problems with possible investors, consultants coming on board and potential clients. Have him spending time putting out slanderous fires instead of focusing on building his new company's brand.

His phone dinged with a reminder for an upcoming meeting. There was so much more he wanted to discuss with Sasha, but the timing of the reminder was perfect. He needed to think.

"That was work. I've got to run." He stood. "Are you going to be okay?"

"I hope so," she replied, standing as well. "Thanks for coming over."

He reached over for her. She stepped into his arms and laid her head on his shoulder. As chaotic as everything was around them, the moment felt right. He still hated that she'd lied to him, but he appreciated her honesty. Hearing more about Sasha's background helped to understand her actions. Not excuse them or justify them but see them from her perspective. He should be here comforting her. She should be in his arms. It was almost as though their story was being written by an unseen hand. Later, there would be time to talk about everything that had happened and the possible consequences. Now she needed support, not judgment. She needed friends, not adversaries. She needed a hero. Jake was available. Only time would tell how the story played out.

Fifteen

Sasha had never been so thankful to work on a project in all her life, and was even more appreciative of the components she'd added and the committee had approved. The many moving parts required her total focus, leaving no room to think about how her life had exploded. The days were full and passed quickly. No time to miss her family's love. No time to stew on Linc's nasty texts. No time to think about her growing feelings for Jake. They hadn't seen each other since he stopped by that Monday. But he'd called every day. As though she were conjuring him up, her phone rang. When she answered, there was a smile in her voice.

"Good morning, Mr. Eddington."

"Good morning, Ms. McDowell."

"I've got like zero time to talk this morning. But I'll give you two minutes."

"I feel special."

"You should."

"You sound better."

"I'm feeling better. Still hurting. Still sad. But still breathing."

"That's always a good sign. What do you have going on today?"

"A meeting with Reign for one thing. When it comes to A-list connections, she's a godsend. Her friend London, the model married to the designer…"

"Ace Montgomery. I know them."

"Well, she accepted a very last-minute request and has graciously agreed to take part in shaping the area of the program helping participants with makeup and style. I'm so excited about that. It will do wonders for their self-esteem. I'm also meeting with the director of a culinary school, a group who own internet businesses and," Sasha scrolled down her list, "a few agencies with clients we want on our guest list. Then I'll have lunch."

"Ha! All that before lunchtime? I'd better get off the phone."

"I can spare another minute. You were also on my to-do list."

"To do what?"

"We've both been incredibly busy. This weekend, I wanted to take you out to dinner to thank you for stopping by on Monday, and discuss everything that happened from the time I arrived in town."

"I can do that."

"Good. Friday or Saturday night?"

"Let me check my schedule and get back with you."

"Okay. Jake?"

"Yes."

"Thanks for calling to check on me. I really appreciate it."

"Not a problem. Linc will most likely never speak to me again, but I'm still watching out for his ex-girl."

Mentioning Linc put a damper on Sasha's mood. She still hadn't heard from family and missed her brothers immensely. Before calling the next agency on her list, she tapped TJ's number.

"Yeah."

The caustic greeting was a glaring sign that he was still very angry. "Hi, TJ. I'm glad you answered this time."

"I almost didn't. You've really gone and screwed things up, Sasha. Lincoln doesn't deserve being treated so poorly. What in the heck got into you?"

"I know that to everyone at the dinner my actions seemed sudden, even irrational. But this latest incident was not our first breakup, only the final one. Trust me, Lincoln and I had spoken about my doubts and feelings many times."

"Then why were you acting like y'all were still together? You were still wearing the man's ring!"

"It's what he wanted, not me. I did it because…because he asked. It was a mistake. I realize that now. To be honest, I also did it because of what I knew would happen. All of you are acting just as I thought you would, taking Lincoln's side without giving me any consideration. Being more concerned with optics than my actual life."

"Don't go trying to throw a pity party now, little sister. You're not the victim here. You date a man for four years and then conveniently dump him after spending time in Chicago with that no-good Jake Eddington who everyone knows chases skirts for sport. You were naïve enough to fall for his game. I thought you were smarter than that."

A lone tear escaped from Sasha's eye. She let it fall and blinked away another. "You know what, TJ? You're my brother and I love you. But we don't know each other anymore. You remember the little sister who you bossed around, the one without a mind of her own. You've never really gotten to know the woman I've become. Contrary to the popular belief of you and the rest of our family, I am very smart. I did think through this decision. I weighed all the options and made the only viable choice. Would you want me in a bad marriage just to make the family look good? Would it matter that I was unhappy, or would you be more concerned with how everyone else felt?"

"You talk like Lincoln's a criminal. He's a good man, Sasha. And like a brother to me and Brandon."

"Exactly. And that is my affection toward him, more like a brother than a husband. Linc and I didn't start dating because of mutual attraction. We started dating because it is what was expected. I do think over time Linc fell in love with me. Unfortunately for everyone, I couldn't return that feeling."

"Are you dating Jake?"

Sasha twirled an errant curl as she pondered her response. "No, but I like him."

"That's your problem, little sister. You don't know what you want."

"I knew I didn't want to spend my life with Lincoln.

We broke up before I came to Point du Sable. Jake has zero responsibility in the choice I made. Still, he's a good man too. You know that, otherwise you wouldn't have asked him to watch out for me."

TJ snorted. "Neither Linc nor I will make that mistake again."

"You won't have to. I can take care of myself. Please tell Mother that I love her and miss her. I hope she'll return my call soon."

Though it was disagreeable, Sasha was still glad to have spoken with her brother. It made her feel connected rather than completely tossed away. She and Val had dinner that evening. Her godmother helped her perspective too.

"You only get one life, Sasha. This is yours. No one can live it for you. No one should. Remember that."

The weekend arrived. With everything for the benefit almost completed, Val joined a few friends for a spa retreat at Hotel Bouvó, a boutique hotel outside Chicago. Sasha declined the invitation. She had other plans. Dinner with Jake. He'd called and confirmed that Friday night would work for him. She dressed with care. A bold, gold, crop-top sweater paired with striped wide-legged slacks and an ankle-length black leather coat to keep out the dipping temps. Her freshly washed and conditioned hair was left in its curly state. She kept makeup minimal but used a sparkly gloss and outlined her eyes in a smoky shadow, a nod to the special night. Jake insisted on picking her up and didn't say where they were going. When he arrived promptly at seven thirty, looking like a modern-day Neo from *The Matrix* in a black leather trench and black wool slacks, she didn't care where they went. Just that they were together.

Once in the car and buckled up, Jake looked at her curiously. "What?"

He tilted his head in her direction and deeply inhaled.

She shrank away. "What. Are. You. Doing?"

"You're wearing it. The cologne you had on that night at the party."

Her eyes widened. "I am."

"Is that why you stopped wearing it after that night, so I wouldn't guess the tigress was you?"

"That would have been clever but, no. I'd sprayed it on before boarding the plane but forgot to pack the bottle. Val has a vast collection and told me to help myself, which I did. You've got a good nose."

"I don't know about all that. Some things you don't forget."

Said in a way that made Sasha think he wasn't just talking about the perfume from that night. Sasha remembered everything about their lone encounter and hoped now that she was single, maybe they could try and capture the magic again.

"I called TJ."

"How'd that go?"

"About as expected. My family can't seem to understand my wanting to be in love with the man I marry."

"They get it. They just want what they want."

"I hope they get over it before next weekend. I don't want that bad vibe at the benefit."

"Your family is coming?"

Jake's question gave her pause. She'd looked forward

to them joining her and even with all that had happened couldn't imagine her family not showing up.

"My mom, TJ and TJ's girlfriend are coming. Oh, gosh. Lincoln's mother, Ruthanne, is supposed to come too!"

"Think she'll still show up?"

"I don't know. I need to call her. I also need to remember to seat your mom and sisters on the other side of the ballroom from my mom and Ruthanne."

"Don't worry. They're all much too classy to take a conflict public. If they run into each other in the bathroom though…"

"Might be a problem?"

"Mona didn't take much back in the day, at least according to Dad."

Sasha giggled.

"What, you think my mom having a fight is funny?"

"No, it's my mom I'm imagining. That scene is not cute!"

"Sounds like you have a few loose ends you need to wrap up."

Sasha sighed. "Yeah."

"Did TJ mention me?"

"Yes."

"What did he say?"

"I'd rather not repeat it."

To her surprise, Jake laughed. "TJ always was an asshole." He paused, gave her a look. "No disrespect. I don't blame him. Linc either. If I thought someone was trying to screw over my sister, or my woman, I'd react the exact same way or worse."

At hearing *my woman* come out of Jake's mouth, Sasha turned all gooey inside.

"This is all so messy."

"It's called life, love."

They reached the restaurant and settled down for a delicious meal. After placing their orders, Sasha spoke.

"Jake, we've discussed this before, but for the record I want to apologize again for deceiving you. Our night together wasn't planned but once I discovered your identity, you should have been told right away. I don't regret one second of what happened, but how I handled the situation afterward was neither honest nor fair."

Sincerity oozed from sparkling brown eyes as she looked at him intently. "Given a second chance, I would handle everything differently. Do you think you can forgive me?"

"Forgiving isn't forgetting you know."

Sasha nodded.

"I wish you'd told me that first Sunday when I asked. Still, I don't think your actions were malicious. You probably did what felt best at the time. This is a tricky, sticky situation but yes, I forgive you."

"Thank you, Mr. Eddington."

"You're welcome, Ms. McDowell."

Their smiles could have lit up a blackout.

Conversation flowed even more freely after that through topics of mutual interest. The atmosphere remained light as they finished dinner.

"What about dessert?"

"I'm stuffed," Sasha said, rubbing her stomach. "Maybe a to-go bag?"

"Sure."

They left the restaurant. Sasha was glad when Jake suggested a nighttime drive through the city. She wasn't ready for the evening to end. Chicago was a scenic city at night, especially when seen from the confines of a cozy, luxury ride. They drove along Lake Shore Drive and the Chicago River, and past Navy Pier, Millennium Park, Buckingham Fountain and other local attractions. Jake took her to the building Cayden had bought Avery, where her business, On Point Event Planning, anchored the first floor. They drove by the sports arenas and Willis Tower, Chicago's tallest building. Somewhere along the way the music shifted from old-school hip-hop to romantic R & B ballads. Their mutual attraction was unspoken, and palpable.

"I'd better get you home," Jake said, after pointing out another landmark. "I don't want Val to think you've been kidnapped."

"No need to worry. She decided to enjoy this relative calm before next week's storm and is spending the night at a hotel and spa."

"Hmm."

"Sounds like a good idea, huh?"

"It does."

Sasha took it a step further. "I could use a massage."

"Are you saying you're not ready for the night to be over?"

She sighed. "I wouldn't be surprised if Linc has PIs on me right now. He's a sore loser who can be vindictive when hurt."

"I found that out."

"How?"

"He made threats," Jake said, without giving details.

"I hope he doesn't follow through with trying to sully my character. I'm not concerned about what society thinks but in business, reputation is paramount."

"Jake, I'm very sorry for having gotten you caught up in all this."

"It's not your fault."

"Not totally, but somewhat."

"Yeah, had I known it was you in the tiger dress, that night would not have happened."

"Are you sorry it did?"

"I wish the timing and circumstances were different. The consulting firm I'm creating is important to me. I love my family and am proud of what Eddington Enterprise has accomplished, but the firm will be my baby, independent of what my father built.

"The world of the one percent, heck even the ten percent, is small. Your father and I are brothers in the Society of Ma'at, and Mr. Trotter as well. That alone causes us to travel in some of the same circles, with the same people. If Linc put out the narrative that I slept with his fiancée and broke up the engagement, it would place me in a negative light with the society, and my family by extension."

"But you didn't sleep with his fiancée. Linc and I had already broken up."

"That's the truth, but in today's world it's the narrative that counts. Perspective matters. If a story line is repeated early and often, a blatant lie can be perceived as the truth. If the collective conscious buys into it, facts no longer matter.

"I'm not disappointed about not working with Linc. Even without the added layer of what happened between us, seeing how he handles himself in stressful situations would have changed my mind about going into business together. He's got a lot of good attributes professionally, but no one wants a hothead on their team. Being with you is not as easy to dismiss. You're a beautiful woman, inside and out. Another time, another place and I'd be all over you, sweetheart. But judging from everything that's happened in the short time we've been around each other, now is not the time for us. It's tough, but that's how it is."

Sixteen

The following week, Jake's words to Sasha haunted him. Shutting down any chance of them dating sounded good at the time but the reality of it felt like crap. He was starting to question that decision, to wonder if the sacrifice of not going after what he wanted was truly the right thing to do. With the upcoming benefit, Sasha's week had been hectic. They hadn't seen each other and talked only once. Texts had kept them connected, but barely. Jake missed her and didn't want to fill his time with anybody else. In short, not being able to act on his feelings for Sasha was becoming a problem. Even with difficult challenges, Jake was known for being a problem solver. But coming up with one that aligned with both his personal and professional goals would not be an easy task.

He put those thoughts aside as he neared the valet stand by the circular drive. His steps were light as he exited his car and walked up the sidewalk to the Point du Sable Country Club entrance. Inside, a plethora of luxuriousness milled around—necks and arms bedazzled with jewels, hands holding flutes of champagne. He spoke to several people as he walked through the crowd looking for Sasha.

"Wow, brother, you look nice!"

Jake turned and smiled as Reign walked toward him. "You don't look half bad yourself." He took her hand and twirled her around. "Did you get that at the fashion show?"

"Sure did. An Ace original."

For Val's benefit, the town had turned out en masse. A guest list reading like a who's who of high society were all there to show their support. The entire Eddington clan was in the building and had purchased half a dozen tables for special clients and company execs.

Jake continued to scan the crowd. "Where's Sasha?"

"She's around here somewhere."

"How's she holding up?"

"Her family didn't come. That has to sting. She's putting on a brave face but her heart is breaking. It's got to be. Thanks in part to her efforts, the earlier portion of the drive was an incredible success. The whole town is buzzing about the great time had at today's events. The workshops were phenomenal and continue tomorrow. I spoke briefly with Mrs. Baldwin, who has already asked Sasha if she'd help again next year."

"I'm glad to hear today went well but wish her family had shown up to support her."

"Me too. She did an awesome job and should be very proud of her work. I'm sure she'll fill you in on all the details, but she was also surprised by receiving a huge honor today. The mayor issued a proclamation and gave her a key to the city. Probably Val's doing but from what I saw, well deserved. The recognition probably uplifted her spirits too. She was glad for our presence, but I can only imagine what it would have meant had her own family been here. For them to treat her this badly for living life on her terms is mind-boggling. It doesn't make sense."

"What doesn't?" Cayden and Avery joined them in the crowded lobby next to the ballroom.

"Sasha's family," Jake replied. "They completely missed the drive and bought a table for the benefit but refused to come. Her ex's family had purchased a table too."

"Are there guests to fill them?" Avery asked. "If not, I can make a call and have that handled ASAP."

"Thanks, Avery," Reign replied. "But Mrs. Baldwin's sorority sisters reached out to a few organizations. Those young ladies you see at the two tables by the wall are the super-excited recipients of the DC ditchers."

"DC ditchers!" Avery chuckled. "That's hilarious."

"Ah, there's Trenton by the bar. I'm going to head over for a glass of wine."

"I think I'll join you."

Avery left with Reign. Cayden turned to Jake. "You think your girl is going to be okay?"

She wasn't his girl, technically, but Jake didn't correct him. In fact, he quite liked the sound of it.

"Sasha's a strong woman. In time, I think she'll be better than ever."

"When is she heading back to DC?"

"I don't think she's planned out that far."

"Avery would love it if she stayed here."

Jake nodded. "I'm sure Mrs. Baldwin would too."

"If she decides to extend her visit and needs a place, let me know. Remember, Mom's condo is empty. She's welcome to stay there for as long as she needs."

"Doesn't she have it listed as an Airbnb?"

"It can be unlisted."

"Thanks, man. I'll let her know."

Cayden's eyes shifted to over Jake's shoulder. "Speaking of…"

Jake turned around. His heart melted. Sasha looked like an angel. Her sparkly white off-the-shoulder number stood out in the crowd. For him, she could have worn jeans and had the same effect. Her hair was swept in an updo, with tendrils dangling around her neck and shoulders, exposing creamy skin that his fingers ached to touch. The angel brought out the devil in him.

He helped close the distance between them, then pulled her into a warm embrace.

"Jake," she whispered. "Let's cool it with the PDA."

"Why? Your family isn't here."

A look of hurt registered. He immediately regretted the remark.

"Sorry, Sasha. That was thoughtless of me to say."

"It's the truth, unfortunately." She took a second to compose herself. Her chin lifted slightly. "A few of Val's soror friends are here from Baltimore, DC's neighbor. I'm sure everything that happens here will get relayed back home. I don't want the Grand Canyon sized chasm between my family and me to grow any wider."

"It's your family's loss. You look absolutely incredible."

Her eyes sparkled as she smiled. "Thank you."

"I hear congratulations are in order. Our mayor doesn't hand out proclamations to just anyone."

Sasha's face flushed. She beamed with pride. "I was shocked, but seriously, it made me happy. I worked very hard to take the benefit to another level. That my effort was recognized meant everything."

"May this be the first of many accolades."

"We'll see."

"Are you still on the clock?"

"Technically, no. On Point is handling this last, celebratory portion of the benefit. Willow and several assistants. Val, myself and the rest of the committee are free to party."

"In that case, let's grab a flute of champagne to toast your success."

Halfway through Sasha's glass of champagne, Val pulled her away from Jake to introduce her to some of Val's special guests. Jake barely spoke to her all evening. Every time he looked up, someone new was garnering her attention. Several eligible bachelors were among them, much to Jake's chagrin. Along with his family, several good friends and clients were in attendance. Jake tried to have a good time. The only person he wanted to be with was in the same ballroom but for all the difficulty in trying to spend a private moment with Sasha, she may as well have been on Mars. Finally, around midnight, as the gala wound down, Jake saw her sitting and texting at a nearby table. He leaped at the opportunity for a few minutes of having her to himself.

"You're a popular lady," he said, sitting down not right beside her but with a chair in between. He hadn't forgotten what she said about Val's Baltimore friends. He didn't want to do anything to jeopardize his business plans or Sasha reuniting with her family.

"I feel like I have names and organization titles coming out of my ears."

"If you're rattled, it doesn't show."

"Showing discomfort isn't allowed."

"Never let them see you sweat?"

"Darling," Sasha teased, adopting her mother's posture and tone. "We don't sweat, we perspire, and then only in the privacy of our boudoir."

Jake's laugh was contagious. Soon a nearly delirious Sasha was in an all-out guffaw.

"Let me guess," he said, after settling down. "Your mother?"

"Mrs. Pamela Renee Johnson McDowell, the first and only."

"I'd say I can't wait to meet her but…"

"You don't want to lie? I understand. I love my mother. She is simply the product of her mother, whose family hails from the highest echelons of Harlem society. Grandmother's haughtiness makes Mom's antics look like a street chick. Carrying on the traditions of society were drilled into her, as she's tried to do with my brothers and me. She hadn't counted on getting a rebel."

"You probably hadn't counted on being one."

"Definitely not." Sasha used dainty, freshly manicured fingers to hide a yawn.

"You're exhausted."

"I am."

"Any chance I can talk you into letting me take you home, maybe stopping for a spiced coffee before you turn in?"

"Not tonight, Jake. I've been up almost twenty-four hours and there's four hours of workshops tomorrow. Once those are over, I'll be able to relax and get some real sleep."

"What about Monday? Let me take you to lunch. There are still a few matters I want to talk with you about."

"That sounds doable, but I probably should check with Val. Some of her guests are staying in town a few extra days. She may include me in their plans."

"When are you going back to DC?"

The shift in Sasha's mood was subtle, but there. "I don't know."

"So long as we get a chance to talk before you leave."

"Text me the address for where you'd like to meet on Monday. If I can't make it, I'll let you know."

Jake wanted another hug but when he rose to leave the table, he settled for a quick squeeze of her shoulder. He looked around and, not seeing his family, decided to call it a night. It proved to be a long one. He tossed and turned, his body on fire. He wanted to be with Sasha, which meant trouble with Lincoln and opposition from her family. Problems neither of them needed. With all that was on the line—his reputation, a potentially uber-lucrative consulting business venture not yet off the

ground and Sasha healing the family rift her breakup
had caused—was their mutual attraction, their con-
spicuous desire to be together really worth the risk?

Seventeen

Val had plans for Monday. As a thank-you to the committee who'd worked tirelessly even before Sasha arrived, she'd chartered a luxury bus to drive them from Chicago to the Pleasant Prairie Premium Outlets in nearby Wisconsin, with Coach, Michael Kors, J.Crew and the like offering steep savings on their brands. On the ride up the ladies were treated to gourmet boxed lunches from one of Val's favorite Indian eateries, bottles of sparkling wine or nonalcoholic juices, and serenaded by a mix of old-school and contemporary pop, hip-hop and R & B. It was a break Sasha hadn't known she'd needed.

For most of her life Sasha moved independently, usually having no more than one or two close friends. She'd never experienced the type of sisterhood felt with

Avery and Reign, or that Val and the committee provided, most of whom had worked with Val since the toy, clothing and food drive's inception. All of whom she'd known for years. There were grandmothers, mothers, some daughters of friends. Each woman boasting a lively personality while sharing opinions, judgments and problems. They spoke openly and candidly. They laughed and gossiped about celebrities and politicians and lives outside their own. Sasha didn't share what was going on in her life, but she listened as the women dissected and diagnosed each other's issues. She soaked up the love.

Into the day filled with sunshine and smiles, sat only one big ugly cloud. Sasha still hadn't heard from her family. Even though she hadn't contacted her close friend Val, Pamela had eyes and ears in all parts of society. Sasha knew her mother had heard all about the success of the drive, and about Sasha receiving an award and city proclamation. That she hadn't called cut deeply. That the family was still holding on to the version of Sasha's life they thought best for her poured unnecessary grief over what should have been a shining moment.

Later that night, Sasha and Val sat covered with fluffy throws drinking chamomile tea.

"I spoke with your mother."

This news was shocking. Sasha put down her teacup. "I didn't think she'd called you."

"She didn't. I called her. As your godmother I felt it my duty to let her know how I felt about your mistreatment, how very proud everyone here is of the work you did and what an amazing opportunity they missed to see their daughter shine."

A flood of gratitude filled Sasha's heart. "You said all that?"

"I sure did, and a few other things that I won't share. I've known Pamela since we were eleven and thirteen years old. I know about parts of her life that others don't. I remember her when she was your age and reminded her of situations and feelings she seems to have forgotten. She can intimidate others, but not me."

"How did she respond?"

"Defensive, but she listened. Deep down, she knows I'm right. I told her she needed to speak with you, immediately, and listen without judgment to what's in your heart."

"Do you think she will?"

"Only time will tell. Meanwhile, you're welcome to stay here as long as you want. You've reached out several times only to be rejected. For what it's worth, when it comes to your family, I think the next move should be on them."

Val's pep talk helped Sasha not mope around but instead put her energy into shaping a future that didn't revolve around her family and was not in DC. Upon Ivy's recommendation she spoke with a holistic therapist. The session lasted two hours. Sasha spoke honestly about her feelings of inadequacy, high family expectations and the trauma of being bullied while living thousands of miles from home. She talked about Lincoln and Jake and the fallout from desiring one over the other. The therapist listened attentively, taking notes and rarely interrupting. At the end of their session, the therapist made productive suggestions, including purchasing a journal to not only daily write down her feelings, but also devise a plan for creating the type of life she wanted. Doing so was very freeing. Only days later, Sasha had made several crucial, life-changing decisions. She would write letters to her mother, father and brothers, final olive branches to her family before she took Val's advice and let the next move be theirs. For now, she would stay in Illinois. Val had offered her home indefinitely, but Sasha decided to look for a condo with a short-term lease. She would not try and hold on to her past life. In two months, her father would be hosting an annual presidential campaign fund-raiser. Not being there would hurt. She would miss the buzz and preparations for an event that had always been looked forward to and enjoyed as a family. Her dad's presidential pledge parties, as informally named, were always grand celebrations with A-list stars. From the venue to the food to the entertainment to the guests—everything was top-shelf and first-class—one of the times Sasha appreciated the perks of being an ambassador's daughter. For the first time since returning from Switzerland, she might not be there. She wouldn't call her family and grovel for one of the outlandishly expensive, six-figure tickets, one that with her newly independent financial status she could hardly afford. Instead she'd decided on using that weekend to return to the city and clear out the condo her parents owned, effectively transferring her life from DC to Chicago. She would also call Ruthanne and request a lunch date. Sasha thought highly of Lincoln's mom and felt she deserved a face-to-face conversation. Finally, Sasha would allow herself to be vulnerable and share her heart with Jake. She couldn't say it was love yet, but whatever she was feeling for him ran deeper and felt stronger than at any other time with any other man. She not only desired him physically, she loved his company. His wit. His style. His swag. She wanted to be around him, and she wanted to let him know.

By the end of the following week, she'd written and sent off the letters. While she was nervous about the outcome, a weight had been lifted. She'd informed them of her decision to remain in Chicago, and that she would be spending the upcoming holidays with Val and her daughter Valencia, who'd return stateside just before Christmas and be in town for three weeks. Jake had been busy, traveling and working on business for both himself and Eddington Enterprise. During this time, they rarely spoke by phone but exchanged texts often. That they stayed connected was enough for Sasha. Jake was more reserved. She sensed there was still a river of unanswered questions between them. She wanted to get to know Jake much better and hoped he felt the same way.

Christmas was different, but lovely. The ache of missing her family was somewhat eased by a video chat that morning, even with the emotional chill still felt in the air. The Trotters were in Barbados, TJ reminded, providing information Sasha didn't need. The McDowells had decided on a quiet affair, the immediate family sans girlfriends. Later, her parents were dining with four other couples. Her brothers planned to meet up with dates. The words weren't spoken but their group wasn't complete. She was missed. They pointed the camera toward a stack of presents. "For when you come back," Brandon said.

At Val's house in Point du Sable, it was just the la-

dies. It had been years, easily a decade, since she'd seen
Valencia but for all the seriousness of her profession,
the doctor was funny, equally knowledgeable on world
events and celebrity gossip, and told great stories. They
bonded over food that they all made together—omelets
and spicy Bloody Marys for their late morning meal and
an Italian-inspired dinner after presents were opened.
All day she thought of Jake. While they'd texted Christmas greetings that morning, she was disappointed he
hadn't called. She told herself it was probably because
of being busy with family. Once dinner was over, however, she was done waiting. She declined an invitation
to join Val and Valencia on a trip to the movies. Once
the house was quiet, she called Jake.

"Merry Christmas, Mr. Eddington!" Sasha worked
to sound lighter than her heart felt.

"Same to you, Ms. McDowell. How was your day?"

She gave a condensed version of the day's activities.
"Val and Valencia just left for the movies," she finished.

"Probably the same new release half of my family is
seeing. At the last minute I decided to join them but the
theater's sold out."

"How was your Christmas, Jake?"

"Very lively. The addition of little ones to the holidays brings back the wonder we all remembered as children. Plus, Mom collects strays and invites them all to
dinner. She makes it her business to have no one spend
their Christmas alone."

"What are you doing now?"

"Heading out for drinks with friends. You?"

"Not sure yet," she answered casually, as her heart
hit her stomach with a thud. Only now she realized a

part of her had hoped they'd get together. Instead he was meeting friends, likely of the female variety. It was his right. He'd told her he didn't think they would work out. That their feelings were right but the timing was wrong. For an emotion that defied logic the facts didn't matter. Sasha was falling for a man who'd moved on.

"Plans for New Year's too?" She probably didn't want to know the answer but couldn't help herself.

"Always a lot of options in a big city," was his non-committal reply.

"I'd love to bring it in with you," she found herself saying, speaking honestly, as she should have before. "Just friends," she added. A total lie.

"If you hear about something fun and not too formal, let me know."

Sasha hung up the phone with a new and unexpected conundrum. She hadn't considered life in this new town without Jake. Val was amazing and Reign, Avery and Willow were becoming friends. Putting on the event with Val had introduced her to a variety of acquaintances. It made for a very small circle, though, and while Val had casually suggested a few of her friends' eligible sons to go out with, the dating game held little appeal.

As New Year's Eve approached, Sasha prepared to do something that hadn't happened before—bring it in alone. A depressing thought, but less so than celebrating and acting happy with a roomful of gleeful, possibly drunk strangers and no one to kiss at the countdown. She decided to use the evening to journal, create a vision board and figure out what she wanted to do with this new life. If she couldn't celebrate with Jake she could at least be productive.

She was in a shop gathering materials for her up-coming private party when her phone rang. Pulling it out and then seeing Jake's number brought out a swirl of emotions.

"Hey, Jake."

"Hello, beautiful. What are you doing?"

"Just a little shopping."

"A woman's favorite pastime."

"Absolutely. What's going on with you?"

"Just relaxing, thinking about New Year's Eve."

Sasha didn't want to get too excited. She reached for a beautiful journal covered with gold leaf and crystals and kept her response low-key.

"Really?"

"Yes. Did you decide what you were going to do yet?"

"I'm having a party."

"And I wasn't invited?"

"It's a party of one." She shared her plans. "It's a new life for me here. I figured what better way to bring in the New Year than with clear goals and a well thought out plan for how to achieve them."

When there was no answer, she looked at her phone. They were still connected. "Jake?"

"Is that what you really want to do?"

"Of my current options, it's the most attractive."

"Would you like us to bring it in together?"

"Only if it's what you truly want."

"There's one thing you should know about me, Ms. McDowell. I only do what I want to do. Nobody forces my hand."

The night arrived. In spite of telling herself it was no big deal and reminding herself of Jake's declaring that their dating was not an option, Sasha was excited. This would be the first time they'd seen each other since their evening in Chicago. When he'd called the night before to make firmer plans, she suggested that he do the choosing. It was his town after all. Neither was interested in attending the annual party and fireworks display at the Point Country Club. Jake had invites to half a dozen swanky parties but attending them came with the chance for unwanted publicity. A private dinner sounded much more their speed. Jake had insisted on doing all the planning. "Dress casual," he'd informed her once they decided. "And bring an overnight bag. No one wants to be on the road on New Year's Eve."

At precisely five thirty, the doorbell rang.

"Do you want me to get that?" Val called from the kitchen.

"Could you please," Sasha responded. "I'm almost ready."

When she entered the living room less than ten minutes later, Jake and Val were laughing and chatting comfortably. He looked yummy in his simple sweater and jeans, a leather jacket thrown over the couch arm. He stood when she entered and gave her a light hug.

"I forget the two of you know each other," Sasha said.

"Mrs. Baldwin and my mother know each other," he corrected. "I'm much more acquainted with her daughter Valencia. She's several years older, but I remember her from years at the club when I tried to hang out with Desmond's crowd."

"I watched all of Mona's kids grow up." She beamed at Jake. "They've all turned into productive, contributing adults. Derrick and Mona did a lot of things right."

She turned to Sasha, took in the oversize sweater paired with skinny corduroy leggings and knee-high boots.

"Pardon me for saying so," Val began. "But the two of you do not look like you're heading to a fancy New Year's Eve celebration."

"We've both had our share of galas this season. Tonight, Jake suggested something low-key, which sounds perfect."

Sasha watched Val's eyes slide from the faux fur coat over her right arm to the overnight bag she wheeled to her left.

"I'm glad the two of you are not letting the expectations of others dictate your lives. Both of you are amazing souls with bright futures. And you make quite the dashing couple."

"Val…" Sasha began.

Val held up a hand. "I'm just saying the two of you look well together. An innocent compliment." Said with a twinkle in her eye that suggested it was anything but.

Jake stepped forward to give Val a hug and a kiss on the cheek. "Thanks, Mrs. Baldwin. I'll take care of Sasha. Will you be bringing in the New Year at the club?"

"Of course, with strict orders for my driver to pick me up at exactly 12:05!"

"Happy New Year, Mrs. Baldwin."

"Happy New Year, Val!"

Jake reached for Sasha's carry-on and led them to the car. Once settled, Sasha asked him, "Where are we going?"

"Chicago."

"Care to be more specific?"

"It's a private residence my brother-in-law owns."

Sasha arched a brow.

"Don't worry. This isn't a planned seduction."

"It isn't? Damn."

They laughed.

Jake reached for her hand, gave it a quick squeeze then released it. "I figured that while the rest of the world partied with loud crowds, you and I can do the opposite, spend a quiet night getting to know more about each other. It might sound boring, but I think you'll like what I have planned."

They arrived at an impressive high-rise, with a doorman, boasting huge blocks of granite and gleaming steel. They took an elevator to one of the higher floors. Sasha's stomach fluttered as they stopped at a pair of double doors at the end of the hall. He used the key card, opened the door and said, "After you."

Sasha walked into a wonderland. Mini white globe lights were everywhere, casting rainbows from the crystal chandeliers onto the off-white furniture that dominated the room. Fragrant orchids and hyacinths filled a myriad of vases in different sizes and shapes. Floor-to-ceiling paneless windows dominated the far wall, providing a postcard view of the sparkling city lights and shimmers off the waters of Lake Michigan. Soft music enveloped them. The fireplace glowed. In the living room were two massage tables and beyond them another table lined with oils, stones and towels.

"A couple's massage?"

"For starters. I remembered you wanting one."

"Nice."

Sasha continued her quick perusal. To the right of the living room was a richly appointed dining room with an elaborate setting for two. There were other hallways and other rooms beyond it but Sasha had seen enough to know she was in for a memorable evening. She walked over and gave Jake a hug.

"This is beautiful, very thoughtful. Thank you." She lifted her face and offered a quick kiss on the lips. It was a risk, but she couldn't help it. She didn't want to come off as presumptive or overly flirtatious. Given Jake's hesitance she needed to tread lightly, even cautiously, to whatever destination awaited. But the kiss was deserved and warranted. Jake had transformed what could have been a night of sadness away from her family into a magical evening.

She motioned toward the dining table set with fine china, crystal goblets, linen napkins and tapered candles in platinum holders. "You said this was going to be casual."

Jake shrugged. "As Mrs. Baldwin pointed out, it is New Year's Eve."

"With all of this beauty, it doesn't feel right to be wearing jeans."

"You're right."

Sasha looked slightly alarmed.

"Don't worry. I've got you."

He absolutely did. When Sasha returned to her bedroom following an incredible massage, it was to a walk-in closet boasting designer boxes and a garment bag hanging in the closet. She unzipped it to reveal a sparkly pink mini with a high neck and long sleeves. Sasha could not have done better had she picked out the dress herself.

In the boxes were shoes, several to choose from and all in her size. She skipped over the enclosed pumps and ankle booties to choose a pair of snazzy stilettos with silky straps that wrapped around her shins. The other boxes held fancy toiletries, jewelry and a large bottle of her favorite perfume. With each box she opened, her resolve to keep tonight platonic weakened more and more. Impatient to give Jake a proper thank-you, she hurried through the bubble bath that had been drawn for her pleasure and before the bell rang announcing dinner, found herself back in the living room, staring out the window and wondering how in the heck this had become her new life.

"Hello, Ms. McDowell."

Sasha slowly turned around and strolled toward Jake with the biggest smile on her face. He looked as handsome as she'd ever seen him, the single-button tailored suit showcasing a god body. His soft curls gleaned; his dark eyes mesmerized her. But it was his lips that drew her to him. She reached him, placed her arms around his neck and kissed him the way she'd wanted to since that night at HalloMask.

Sasha felt Jake practicing restraint. It didn't last long. She leaned her body into his hard chest, crushed her breasts against him, allowing the soft, silky fabric of the dress to create a current between them. Her tongue swiped his lips, demanding entry. With a sigh he obliged, enveloping her with his arms and pulling her closer. His hands were everywhere. Her hair. Shoulders. Lower back. Ass. Their tongues touched and swirled and made their reacquaintance. Sasha was hungry but not for what was set to be served in the dining room.

She wanted Jake. Here. Now. She didn't want to wait a moment later.

Jake broke the kiss. They stood there breathless, wanting, bodies on fire. Jake adjusted the evidence of his desire, his eyes smoldering as he gazed at her.

"Dinner is in five minutes," he managed. "John has worked on this for hours. It would be a shame to let it go to waste or have to heat it up later."

"Okay."

"You are hungry, aren't you?"

Sasha gave Jake's body a shameless once-over before running her hand across the bulge in his slacks.

"I have a voracious appetite."

Jake swallowed. He reached for her hand. "Then let's not keep the chef waiting."

As if on cue the family chef, John, appeared at the dining room entrance. "Mr. Eddington. Ms. McDowell. Dinner is served."

Eighteen

A private home. That gorgeous dress. What had he been thinking? A myriad of thoughts vied for Jake's attention as he placed a hand at the small of Sasha's back and guided them into the dining room. When he'd seen her standing at the window, her curvy silhouette outlined against the city lights wearing a dress that looked to be made solely for her body, he'd barely been able to contain himself. He'd wanted to go over, rip off that pricey number and claim her body as his. He wanted to make love to her, fast and frenzied and then slow and easy. He wanted to kiss away all of her hurt, lick away every bad memory, thrust away every ounce of anger that may have remained. But he didn't. As much as he wanted to be with Sasha intimately, there were still a great deal of obstacles between them. He'd jumped into her bed blindly that night back in October. He would use every ounce of discipline it took to not make that same mistake again.

They reached the dining room to find elegant menus printed with gold ink on cream-colored linen paper. They sat and read quietly, the chef waiting a few unobtrusive feet away.

"John, you've outdone yourself. Everything sounds scrumptious. Sasha, do you agree?"

"Absolutely. The descriptions alone make my mouth water."

"Then I shall bring your first course. But first," he walked over to where a bottle of champagne chilled in a bucket, "may I offer the first pour of the evening? Jake, these bottles are from the exclusive Drake Wines collection. Only a few hundred exist in the world."

"Thank you for choosing this occasion to open a couple. Like their product, I do believe this evening will be one-of-a-kind."

Over an amuse-bouche of perfectly seared scallops topped with Karelian Kaluga caviar and toasted sesame seeds, followed by a chilled peanut soup and microgreens salad, Jake's and Sasha's ardor cooled. The champagne flowed. They both relaxed. Comfortable conversation followed. They talked about Val's event, Jake's travels, how each had spent Christmas. Finally, Jake felt the ground beneath them stable enough to bring the conversation around to Sasha, and them.

"I have an idea," he said, before downing a smoked oyster dusted with spices. "Maybe you should move away from DC, start fresh, get a new perspective."

Sasha looked up coyly. "Got any particular place in mind?"

"Hell, yeah. Here, Chicago. More specifically, Point du Sable."

"Why do you think that would be a good idea?"

Jake reached for his water goblet. "PDS is a great place to live. Small community, a bit gossipy. But you never meet a stranger and everyone helps everyone else. It's right next to Chicago, arguably one of the best cities in the Midwest. There are people here who care a great deal about you. Val was very impressed with your work. According to Cayden, Avery would love for you to join her event planning business."

"What about you? Are you one of those people who care a great deal about me?"

"I've been attracted to you from the moment we met, before the masks came off and I knew you were you. I'd never want to come between you and your family. I'd like to speak with Linc man-to-man. But yes, Sasha, what happens to you matters to me. I know I said it wasn't possible. But if you were here, and available, I'd love for this to not be our last evening out."

"I'd love that too." Sasha's eyes sparkled with relief. "I went to see a therapist."

"How'd that go?"

"Quite productive, actually. She helped me make some rather major decisions. I wrote letters to my family and put the ball in their court. And just yesterday, I decided to attend a prestigious annual presidential fund-raiser hosted by my father, something that because of the cost, but mainly out of fear and the rift with my family, I was not going to do. It's a major event in DC, especially for networking. Whatever I plan to do professionally, contacts are key. Plus, it's one of my favorite events."

"Those were not easy decisions, babe. I'm proud of you."

"Thank you. I felt pretty good, too, especially about the most critical decision." She paused. "Moving to Chicago."

A slow smile spread across Jake's face. "You had me do all of that selling when you'd already made up your mind."

"I wanted to hear your argument."

"How was it?"

"Very convincing."

"Do you think you'll stay with Val?"

"I want my own place."

"I might be able to help with that." Jake told Sasha about Cayden's offer. "Or," he added, looking around them. "If you'd feel better living in the city, I might be able to work something out with Victor, Maeve's husband, so that you can stay here."

"In this phenomenal property? I couldn't imagine." She looked around. "Well, then again, actually I could."

"I'll see what I can do."

"Don't bother. I'd never be able to afford it."

"Did I mention anything about rent?"

Sasha shook her head. "That's a generous offer, Jake, but I can't accept it. I just got out of a relationship with a man who tried to control me. Not saying that's you," she hurried on before he could argue. "You're nothing like Linc. I just want everything about this next chapter of my life to be of my own choosing, and my own making. Sink or swim, win or lose, I want all of the responsibility to be mine."

"Cayden's mother's condo would be much more affordable, and an arrangement made directly between you and Tami, his mom."

"I'd be happy to speak with her about it. PDS is an impressive town. But I think Chicago might be more my speed."

Conversation slowed as John served up the entrée—succulent Kobe beef medallions atop beds of Israeli couscous, shaved brussels sprouts, seared tomatoes and morels.

Halfway through the entrée, Jake reached for his napkin. "There's one more thing I think you should know about."

"What's that?"

"I plan to officially rescind the business proposition I gave to Linc."

"You haven't already?"

"Not in writing."

"That shouldn't be a problem, should it?"

"Only if he goes through with his threat of throwing mud on my name by saying I slept with his fiancée and broke up y'all's engagement."

Sasha was immediately livid. "He wouldn't dare. That's a lie and he knows it!"

"Yes but remember it's the threat he used to try and make sure our relationship never went past friendship."

"I'll talk to him, Jake. I'll talk to my brothers. And my parents. They may not like that we've separated but they won't stand by and let Linc tell an outright lie."

"I didn't share my intentions for you to take action.

This is something between Linc and me, something I need to handle man-to-man. Next week, once the holidays are over, I plan to reach out to him for a meeting. I want us to be able to have an honest, civilized conversation. I want to date you, Sasha. I won't sneak around to do it. I won't hide you as though you're something to be ashamed of. You are a jewel who deserves to shine. I just want to be the man catching some of that dazzling light."

John quietly appeared at the dining room entrance.

"If I may, sir. Dessert has been plated, as per your request. The kitchen is cleaned. Everything's back in its place. Both the refrigerator and pantry are stocked. The wine rack is full. Whatever you'll need for the next few days is at your fingertips.

"You didn't ask, but I prepared a breakfast casserole that only needs to be heated. Also, there are strips of tonight's beef in the refrigerator, along with tortillas and toppings for either tacos, enchiladas or a hearty salad."

"As always, John, you've outdone yourself on the food preparation and gone above and beyond my requests for the evening. You're free to go and be able to welcome in the New Year with your lovely wife."

John checked his watch. "Eleven o'clock. Perfect. Thank you for the thoughtful gift of that fancy nearby hotel room you reserved. My wife is ecstatic."

"You are both welcome. Happy New Year."

"If there's nothing else, may I wish the two of you a pleasant remainder of your evening and also the best and brightest in the coming New Year."

The chef left. The masseuses were long gone. Jake and Sasha were alone. Instantly, the atmosphere changed.

"Should we eat our dessert by the fireplace?" he asked.

Sasha's expression conveyed a message that suggested John's molten dark chocolate and vanilla cream concoction could wait. Or be licked off Jake's naked body. But she continued to play along.

"If you'd like."

"Would you like a coffee with it?"

"Sure."

"Then get up, woman, and join me in the kitchen! Did you think I was going to serve you like the Queen of the Nile?"

Again, the sexual tension broke. Sasha followed Jake into the kitchen, fired up the Keurig machine and made them coffees. Jake turned theirs into adult drinks by adding chocolate-and-caramel liqueurs. They sat on a love seat, their bodies touching, with views of both the fireplace and the cityscape scene.

"My God, Sasha," Jake moaned after taking the first bite. "I think whatever John calls this dessert might be better than sex."

"You think so? Let's find out!"

"You've turned from a tigress to a temptress."

"And you just turn me on. Period. I haven't had sex since we were together before." She placed a bite of the dessert on her finger, then stared into Jake's eyes while licking it off.

"Damn, you're sexy."

She placed another bite on her finger and held it out to Jake who did what she had done. His eyes narrowed. His manhood bulged. He reached for his saucer, swiped a dab of the vanilla cream and spread it on Sasha's lips.

Sasha repositioned herself so that Jake's body halfway covered hers as he began to slowly swipe her mouth with his tongue.

Sasha took over. She pushed Jake away from her, straddled his lap and unbuttoned his shirt. He took it off and pulled off his tee. Sasha reached over for a dab of cream and spread it across his chest, and on his nipples. While slowly grinding her hips against him, she licked the cream from his body before pulling his bead of a nipple into her mouth.

"Ah!"

Jake placed his hands on Sasha's thighs, easing the silky dress over her hips to reveal a creamy expanse of skin. The wisp of a thong was no deterrent. He slid his hand between her legs and slipped his third finger into her heat.

She gasped, abandoning his chest and then finding his lips. They kissed with a languid, sultry rhythm. Sasha paused only long enough to pull her dress over her head and fling it to the floor. The lacy pushup bra emphasized her weighty globes, her taut stomach, her shapely hips. Her mouth hungrily searched for his. He expertly released the front-closing clasp and with it, her girls. The firelight played across her skin. And then, so did he. His tongue suckled her nipples into pebbled bliss. His fingers ran along every crevice, encircling her flowers—front and back. Sasha slid her hand between them and massaged Jake's hardened shaft through his clothes.

He was on fire. Only Sasha could put it out.

"Sasha. Move over."

She shifted to allow Jake the freedom to stand. He

quickly removed his shoes and slacks. Sasha kept on her stilettos and the thong. Bathed in dimmed lighting, she looked like a goddess, a nymph. She'd cast a spell and Jake was gladly under it. Nothing to do now but enjoy the ride. He placed a condom on the table but it wasn't time for that yet. Pulling Sasha down onto the love seat, he got on his knees and placed his face in her crotch. Using his tongue he swept aside the lacy triangle covering her femininity and eased his wet tongue between her equally dewy folds. Over and again he licked her, sucked her pearl, slid a finger into her anus.

"So...so...so good," Sasha panted, her hips moving faster as a climax approached. "Oh my God. Jake!"

She went over the edge.

Jake longed to join her there. He secured the condom, then lifted a throbbing Sasha from the love seat and walked them to a wall. Holding her against it in the perfect position, he eased his girth into her heat with excruciating slowness only to pull out to the tip and take the journey again. Sasha's legs wrapped around him. She tried to rush the dance, but Jake wouldn't be hurried. For months, he'd waited for this moment. He wanted to savor every drop. He stepped away from the wall and then, using his strength, slid her up and down his shaft. Sasha moaned and thrashed about, taking in every inch of him, using her muscles to hold him deep within her, cupping his ass to try and take him deeper still.

They moved from the wall to the floor, to the dining room table. Eventually, they made their way to the master suite's king-size bed. He kissed her dragonfly tattoo, outlined it with his tongue.

"I love this. It's how I knew I could correctly identify my tiger."

Sasha turned and stroked his penis. "I love this."

Returning the oral favor, she licked Jake's dick as though it were a rare treasure before easing her lips down his shaft. Her tongue spiraling around his mushroom tip. Her hands caressing his sacs. Jake ran his hands through her soft, silky curls. He pulled out the pins and brought her updo down and around her shoulders, the hair tickling his thighs, making his shaft even harder.

He let her take the lead for as long as he could. But feeling himself begin to lose control, he pulled her to his side, lifted her leg and thrust himself inside her. The feel of her soft ass against him forced him to quicken the pace. He lost himself inside the moment, one he could easily see lasting forever. He thrust and pushed and christened her walls. She swirled her hips and lifted her leg higher. Deeper he went. Harder she grinded. Faster and faster until the world shattered into a million pieces. Jake experienced a massive orgasm. Sasha's was the second of the night.

He fell back against the luxurious mattress and pulled Sasha into his arms.

"That was so good, baby," he told her.

"So, so good," she agreed.

As their breathing slowed and returned to normal the sound of fireworks pierced their lover's cocoon. They turned to see bursts of color lining the sky and heard firecrackers going off in the distance.

Jake kissed Sasha tenderly and held her close. "Happy New Year, Ms. McDowell," he whispered.

"Thank you, Mr. Eddington." She kissed him back. "Happy New Year."

Nineteen

For Sasha, something magical happened that night. That next week, her world looked different. She felt different. Whatever feelings she had for Jake were nothing like she'd ever experienced with anyone else. She still missed her family. She still felt bad about Linc. But for the first time since the final breakup with him, Sasha knew she would be okay.

They'd spent the whole next day at Victor's place in Chicago—eating, talking, making love. Thanks to Jake's super sex skills, Sasha felt liberated and thoroughly satisfied. It had been a long time since she'd had a reason to feel good about herself based on something she'd done, a feat she'd accomplished by working with Val. Spending time with Jake, post-Lincoln, really amplified how much of her life had been spent pleasing others, living up to others' standards instead of her own. Receiving the mayor's proclamation and award had restored Sasha's confidence, rebuilt self-esteem eroded from years of being bullied in school. With the part she'd played in the food, clothing and toy drive's success, along with the therapy that gave her the strength to stand up to her family, the need to please was being exorcised from her system. She'd navigated portions of the world by herself since she was fourteen years old. But taking an original idea from conception to reality, with her opinion being honored rather than questioned, praised rather than criticized—that was new and different. Sasha decided she quite liked it.

She stretched and thought about how quickly her life had changed, how much brighter it was with Jake in it. The Eddingtons were a beautiful family, and not just in a photo op. She hadn't spent much time with Desmond or Maeve, but she considered both Reign and Avery her newest friends. Later, she'd meet them just to hang out. With the time between then and now there was important business to handle. Ideally, it would have been handled in person, but she wanted these conversations behind her. She reached for her phone and dialed a number, holding her breath as she waited for the call to be answered.

"Good afternoon!"

"Ruthanne, it's me. Sasha."

There was a pause as Sasha imagined Ruthanne composing her features. In many ways she and Sasha's mother were opposites but in matters of decorum, they were the same.

"Hello, Sasha. How are you?"

"I'm…okay. How are you?"

"I'm fine. What can I do for you?"

"I just wanted a chance to speak with you one-on-one, to let you know how much I've always admired you and tell you how sorry I am that the engagement between Linc and I didn't turn out as you'd hoped."

"Life is filled with surprises, Sasha. I admit that breakup was one. But Lincoln is young and handsome, smart and driven. He'll meet and marry another woman who can give him the love he deserves."

"I truly believe that, Ruthanne. It's why I couldn't go through with the marriage. Linc is a good man who deserves a woman who loves him in every way. I'll always care for him. We practically grew up together. Our families are still connected. I'd like to think that when seeing each other we can be cordial, maybe in time, even friends."

"Why of course we'll be cordial. How else would we be?"

"Mother and I still haven't talked much."

"Pamela is one of the most stubborn and prideful women I've ever met. She was crushed when plans changed and she wasn't able to orchestrate the wedding of the year as she'd dreamed yours would be. Give her time. She loves you. Your father loves you. TJ and Brandon too. You have a right to be happy, Sasha. I wish you the best."

Ruthanne's words were extremely comforting. Her mood brightened even more. Sasha ended the call and jumped into the shower, ready to have a fun afternoon with Avery and Reign.

On the way out the door, the phone rang. Sasha's eyes

widened when she saw the ID. She tossed her purse on a table and took the nearest chair.

"Mother, hi."

"Hello, Sasha."

"This is... I'm...glad to hear from you."

"At the end of the day I'm still your mother."

Sasha swallowed a mouthful of emotion. "I'm still the daughter who loves you very much."

"Your dad and I received the correspondence you sent. And your brothers."

"You read them?"

"Of course we did. Our Christmas chat wasn't the time to discuss the serious matters they contained."

"I heard that emotions were sometimes best expressed in writing. I thought I'd try it."

"The strategy was successful. You have been heard. We have decided to accept your decision to end the engagement. We are not pleased. I, for one, believe it is a huge mistake. But you are the one who will have to endure the consequences your actions have caused."

"Thanks, Mother. I'm glad that the family has accepted my decision. I spoke with Ruthanne earlier. She seemed to understand and wished me the best."

There was an uncomfortable silence. Sasha realized that as much as she felt her mother didn't really know her, Sasha didn't know Pamela. She didn't know the woman outside her roles as mother and society wife. But she believed her mother loved her, and showed it in the ways that she could.

"One of the reasons I called is regarding the March fund-raiser that your dad does every year. We're delighted to have secured several A-list celebrities and performers for the evening. Of course, all of Washington will be on display. We're hoping that you'll have returned home by then and be able to attend."

So her mother had accepted the broken engagement, but not all of Sasha's plans. The call was going too good for Sasha to point out the error.

"I wasn't sure I'd be invited. It's one of my favorite DC events. I'd love to be there."

"The Trotters will be at our table."

Sasha's shoulders slumped. There it was. The nearly imperceptible prodding, the gentle manipulation.

"Will Linc be there?"

"Isn't he always?"

"Mother, I don't think—"

"Sasha, our families have socialized together for decades. You and Lincoln grew up together. You said so yourself. We've accepted the breakup. Lincoln has as well. I don't think it's too much to ask of you to sit at a table, enjoy a wonderful meal and contribute to casual conversation. When will you arrive back in DC?"

"I will fly in that Saturday."

"You'll be in Point du Sable until March?"

"Yes." As was clearly stated in the letter.

"Val mentioned how successful the event was, and that your efforts were recognized. After reading your letter, your father called and spoke to his good friend Bill Brooks."

"The mayor spoke highly of Father."

"According to Thomas, he also spoke quite highly of you."

"He did?"

"Is that why you're still there, to continue helping Val with her charity work?"

Sasha checked her watch and jumped up from the chair. "That and perhaps other employment. I'm on my way to spend time with a couple friends, one of whom owns an event planning company. They also assisted with Val's event and want to speak with me about joining the team."

"You're trying to get a job?" Asked as though Sasha was plotting to secure illegal drugs.

"I loved working on Val's event. I'm good at that type of planning."

"My goodness, Sasha. What are you doing? Why are you making life difficult by lowering your standards? Working a nine-to-five job is not who you are!"

"I have to run, Mother. Tell Father and the brothers hello. Perhaps I'll arrive on Friday instead of Saturday so that you and I can have lunch."

"We'll see. Goodbye, Sasha."

On the drive to the Point Country Club, Sasha replayed a lifetime of conversations with her mother. Most were with Pamela in the role of a demanding, exacting taskmaster, long on opinions and judgment but short on compassion. There were few times she could recall her mother's encouragement or praise. Sasha's excellent grades and successes were expected, actions that didn't warrant a "job well done."

As a child, Pamela's role had been to mold her into the perfect student and debutante. During her high school years she was the ambassador's daughter, called on to serve as the perfect, charming hostess or the attentive, effervescent guest. Once she and Lincoln began dating, Pamela began her bridal boot camp, demanding Sasha perfect the position of society wife. It was always about the right friends or the right club. The right outfit. The right husband to fit in to their heavily structured, high-profile life. Sasha realized that while meaning well and done for what she thought the right reasons, her mother had been as much a drill sergeant as her military father. Sadly, she realized something else. Pamela McDowell had been Sasha's first bully. It was a startling revelation. But all of that was over now. She was no longer uncertain, or afraid. Like a caterpillar turned butterfly, Sasha McDowell was metamorphosing into a self-sufficient woman who knew who she was, and what she wanted. And even though she felt Jake would be a willing knight more than able to protect her, Sasha knew that in every way that mattered, she could take care of herself.

Twenty

Jake never saw himself as being a one-man woman. Not until at least forty or forty-five. He was fine being the fun uncle, with a choice group of fine and willing females in various parts of the globe with which to frolic and play. Sasha had changed all that. In the two months they'd been officially dating, she'd been more than enough to capture his interest and satiate his hearty sexual appetite. She was intelligent, a required quality, unpredictable, which he liked, and not clingy, a trait he detested. Everyone in his family loved her. She fit in. She fit him.

In his mind, there was only one problem. Lincoln Trotter. His unresolved presence cast a shadow over dating Sasha. They weren't hiding, exactly, but so far they'd maintained a low profile. Quiet dinners. Concerts. Movies. Private events at the club. For Valentine's Day weekend, they'd flown with Reign and Trenton to California in the company jet, joining fashion icons Ace and London Montgomery, and one of Jake's society brothers and his wife for an unforgettable weekend in Malibu. Sasha was renting the PDS condo from Tami, but they spent a great deal of time at Victor's place in Chicago, which held fond memories and had fewer prying eyes.

It was the overhanging threat that rankled. So far, Lincoln hadn't made good on it by spreading false rumors, but Jake still needed to do as he'd planned—have Maeve draw up something legal, put their parting in writing. Jake had good, solid experts ready to come on board and connections with coaches from every major sport. Used wisely, these contacts alone could provide a steady chain of clients for years to come. It would only take one wrong comment, however, one bad mood for Lincoln to change his mind and do something stupid. Something that could cause these months of hard work—networking, strategizing, crisscrossing the country—to crumble around him.

Something else bothered him too. Sasha was attending an event in DC where the McDowells and Trotters would share the same table. Lincoln would be there, likely providing optics that suggested the two were back together—or had never parted depending on how much one knew. Sasha had capitulated to her mother's demand. Their truce was still so tenuous she hadn't wanted it jeopardized. Jake understood, and had suggested his family also buy a table so that he could be

nearby. Sasha had worried about her family's reaction.
And Lincoln's.

"Damn that," Jake growled, abruptly rising from his
office chair and striding toward his cell phone. Sasha
may have to toe a line of societal behavior, but Jake
would not allow himself to be controlled. He scrolled
down the list of contacts on his phone and angrily
punched a number. Then he took a deep breath and
forced himself to calm down.

"What in the hell do you want?"

Jake ignored Linc's rude greeting. He was on a mis-
sion and would not be deterred. "I might have some
business up your way next week and was hoping that
while there you and I could meet."

"Why?"

"Because we need to have a conversation."

"What about?"

"Sasha."

"I'm not going to talk to you about her."

"Okay, then just listen."

Jake waited, half expecting Lincoln to end the call.
When he didn't, Jake continued.

"I never betrayed you with Sasha. She told me the
two of you had broken up before she arrived here. Still, I
kept my distance because the news wasn't public. There
was a chance the two of you would get back together.
Was I attracted to her? Yes. She felt that way too. As we
spent more time around each other, we grew more comfortable—teasing, joking around, like what your cousin
observed at the party. I felt bad, even though technically
the two of you weren't together. Then I saw the Wizards
game and the two of you on national television. From

that moment until she returned after Thanksgiving, my actions toward her were of those to someone engaged."

There was silence as Jake imagined Lincoln absorbing what had been said. "And now?"

"We had dinner together on New Year's Eve and began dating after that."

"Good for you."

"Linc, man, I respect you. Your business skills are impressive. We travel in some of the same circles. I don't want there to be animosity between us and I damned sure don't want any lies surfacing that disparage my name."

"Now we get to what this is really about. Well, if you want any assurances that I won't tell key people what really happened, how you and Sasha really got together, don't hold your breath. In fact, over the holidays I met an internationally popular blogger who'd love to get the exclusive on premium dirt like this—a member of the influential Eddington clan sleeping with the engaged daughter of a US ambassador and breaking up a relationship that lasted for years."

"There's a name for dirt like that. It's called slander. Put that story out there and it won't be me who's ruined. After my attorneys get through with you it will be your family picking up the tattered pieces of a reputation smashed to bits."

"Now who's issuing threats?"

"Not a threat, Lincoln. A promise."

"You don't scare me."

Perhaps not, Jake thought, but the subdued tone in Lincoln's voice did not match his words.

"I'll be honest with you, Linc. Seeing this side of you

has surprised me. I really looked forward to our working together. Of course, that's no longer possible. My attorneys are drafting up a formal dissolution of our prescribed joint venture. You'll get it next week. And just in case you want to try and sabotage that as well, remember the NDA you signed. It's ironclad."

Later that night, he shared the conversation with Sasha.

"I've caused such disruption in your life," she said once he'd finished. "Despite his shortcomings in other areas, Lincoln is an astute businessman."

"That he is."

"Now I've cost you that partner."

"It's okay. I already have someone else in mind."

"Already? Who?"

"Your brother."

"I don't think TJ would be interested. He and Linc are close."

"Not TJ. Brandon. Do you think he'd be open to speaking with me about it?"

"Maybe, and he's such a great guy. In many ways, he and TJ are opposites. Brandon is methodical and level-headed. He's quiet, extremely observant and graduated at the top of his class."

"Cornell, right? With an MBA in economics."

Sasha looked surprised. "What did you do, a background check?"

"That's next week."

She was about to be appalled until she realized he was joking. "And mine after his?" she teased.

Jake kissed her temple. "You've already been cleared.

I plan to attend the presidential fund-raiser," he continued after a companionable silence. "I trust you, Sasha. I don't trust Linc."

"I'm not sure, Jake, especially considering this recent conversation. I understand why you called him. I just wish you'd waited until after Father's event."

"It felt like I was keeping you a secret. I didn't want to wait anymore."

"We've gone out publicly. We're not hiding."

"Not exactly, but Lincoln's ghost continues to hover over us. Otherwise you'd have no problem with me coming to DC." He opened his arms. "Are you angry?"

"No." She cuddled against him. "I just want the evening to be flawless as always. Father is a perfectionist. I don't want to be a part of anything going wrong."

"Is the event sold out?"

"Technically, but there are always a few tables held back for celebrities, dignitaries and other prominent last-minute guests."

"What if I were one of those prominent last-minute additions?"

"You know I love being with you. It's just that…"

"What? You don't trust me?"

Sasha looked at him, her smile bittersweet. "Just as you said earlier, I don't trust Lincoln. My family would also disapprove."

For the next week, Jake and Sasha spent a lot of time together. That Friday, he offered to drive her to the airport. Their parting was tinged with an indefinable feeling.

"I'm going to clear out the condo and be back Wednesday," Sasha offered. "You'll hardly have time to miss me."

That should have been true, but it wasn't. In just a few short months, Sasha had become a very important part of Jake's life.

That night, he strolled past the wide, silk-covered walls of the estate in search of distraction. Hearing muffled voices, he crossed the expansive living space that separated the east and west wings and took a circular staircase down to the lower floor where he soon discovered his dad, Derrick, and brother, Desmond, engaged in a game of chess. He crossed the room and plopped down in one of several swivel chairs.

"Where is everybody?"

"Out," Derrick said, without looking up.

Jake tsked. "Got that part."

"Ivy is having dinner with her mom," Desmond offered, regarding his wife. "Everyone else is in Chicago attending a play."

Jake sighed, got up to get a bottle of water from the mini fridge and heavily sat down again. Another sigh.

This time his dad looked over. "Want to talk about it?"

"Not really." Jake took a swig of water, tried to gather the words that had been swirling around for the past two days about the situation with Sasha and put them together in a way that made sense.

Desmond sat back, gave an imperceptible nod to his father and reached for his Scotch. "Obviously, this is about Sasha."

"Yeah."

"What is it, son? I thought she broke up with her fiancé."

"She did, but..."

Derrick frowned. "But what?"

"It's complicated. Her family didn't agree with the decision. They had other plans and stopped speaking to her for a while."

"Do they know about you?"

Jake looked at his father. "TJ suspects it. But Lincoln knows for sure."

"Lincoln Trotter, right?" Desmond asked. "Weren't the two of you working on something together?"

"We'd discussed the possibility. But that door has closed."

"Better get something in writing, son."

"Already on it, Dad. The paperwork will be sent via special messenger next week."

"Why did you feel the need to speak with him about Sasha?" Desmond asked.

"He's tried to paint the picture that Sasha cheated on him. But she and I got together after they'd broken up. I wanted to eliminate all excuses of ignorance he could try and claim later and make sure that he knew the truth."

"That was rather noble of you, son, but who Sasha is dating is no longer her ex's business."

Jake gave a brief rundown of what had happened. The secret breakup. The very public KissCam moment, Sasha officially ending it all. Her parents threatening to disown her. Linc's initial interest in being a business partner and later, the threats. The only part he left out was the fated night they shared in October, one that he and Sasha decided would remain their secret.

"Did you warn him about what happens to those who try to come against our family?"

"I strongly suggested that was a road he didn't want to go down and if he did, a pack of our lawyers would be there to greet him."

"Led by our sister," Desmond said with a grin.

"Exactly, and best believe, that man wants no part of Maeve."

"Or her husband."

"Dynamic Duo."

Derrick chimed in. "And deadly, if need be."

"Why was her family so set on Sasha marrying Trotter?" Desmond asked, the chess game momentarily forgotten. "I know her father has an influential position and is an authority in Washington, but unless one of her brothers is entering politics, that wouldn't be a huge power union."

"You know, I never thought about that. TJ never mentioned it outright, but I can definitely see him going that route. It could be why he has been such an advocate for Lincoln. Perhaps he wasn't thinking only of Sasha's future, but his as well."

"Have they seen your resume? Sasha hasn't lost anything by dating you instead of Lincoln. I'd say the woman leveled up."

"Thanks, Dad."

"So why are you sitting here as though your dog just died?"

"Her father has a major event this weekend, one

that's held every year. Sasha's attending to try and make peace with her family. But I don't feel good about it."

"Why not?" Desmond asked.

"Because the Trotters, including Linc, will also be there, sharing a table with the McDowells. They're life-long friends. Sasha thinks it's an underhanded move by her mother to get the two of them back together. She assures me she can handle the situation and I believe her. Still, I wanted to be there. She didn't think that was the best idea."

"Is it a private event?"

"No."

"Then why aren't you going?"

"I don't want to do anything to hurt Sasha or give Lincoln a reason to make good on his threat."

"We don't walk to the beat of another man's drum, son. And we never, ever, let anyone or anything get in the way of something we want to be ours."

Jake spent the rest of the evening hanging out with his dad and brother. Their advice was sound and made him feel less helpless than he had when he walked in the room. Once back in his wing of the house, he made a series of phone calls. The last one was to Sasha's god-mother, Val.

"Good evening, Mrs. Baldwin. It's Jake Eddington."

"Jake, my goodness, this is a surprise. I thought you knew Sasha was out of town this weekend. She men-tioned you taking her to the airport."

"I know she's in DC. That's why I'm calling."

"Oh?"

"Yes. I just purchased a table to her father's fund-raiser and wanted to invite you to be my plus-one."

On Saturday night, at exactly 7:55 p.m., five minutes before the dinner was to officially begin, a group
of distinctive-looking, designer-clad individuals entered
the ballroom. Even among this upper-crust crowd, they
stood out. The Eddingtons had shown up en masse and
cut quite a swath as they made their way to one of the
premium tables near the front of the raised dais. Jake led
the way behind the man escorting them to the table, a
dashing figure in his expertly tailored, double-breasted
navy suit, with a tie appropriately striped in red, white
and blue. Filling out the table for ten were Derrick and
Mona, Desmond and Ivy, Reign and Trenton, Avery and
Cayden and Val. Were they not in Costa Rica attending
a best friend's wedding, Maeve and Victor would have
been there too. Jake scanned the room and quickly spotted the McDowells and the Trotters a few tables over.
Sasha's face was turned away from him as she engaged
in conversation with the woman beside her. TJ noticed
Jake first and got Sasha's attention. Jake couldn't hear
what was said, of course, but their expressions told him
two things. TJ wasn't happy to see him. Sasha was.
Surprised, but from the look in her eyes, also pleased,
an assumption further strengthened by the smile now
splitting her face.

She excused herself from the table and came over.
"Hello, everybody!" She walked to Val first, and gave
her a hug, then went around the table until returning
to Jake.

"Hi."

"Hello."

"You're here."

"In the flesh."

"You brought Val!"

"I figured you'd be glad to see her."

She lowered her voice. "That your entire family would support you like this, support us, is awesome." She reached for his hand. "Come. It's time you met my parents. Val, can you join us? Mother will be thrilled at this unexpected surprise."

"I'm not sure thrilled is the word I'd use," Val murmured, as she rose. "But I'll be your bridge over any troubled waters of the Pamela kind. Don't you worry yourself about that!"

It seemed that dozens of eyes followed the three as they walked toward the McDowells' table. There was a subtle change in Pamela's expression as she laid eyes on Jake, but when she noticed it was Val walking beside him, her face lit up.

She stood. "Val! What are you doing here?"

"I was given the opportunity to come and see one of my besties and couldn't pass that up. Have you met Jake Eddington?"

"No," Pamela said, in an even tone, still eyeing Jake. "But I've certainly heard my share."

"We can't always believe what we hear," Val countered smoothly. "Jake Eddington, this is Mrs. Pamela McDowell. Pamela, this is Jake."

"Mrs. McDowell, I can easily see where your daughter gets her beauty. It is a pleasure to meet you."

Clearly struck with the Eddington Edge, Mrs. McDowell's voice held firm but her face softened. "We'll see."

Jake turned to the man now standing beside Pamela. He gave a secret sign known to society brothers. "Ambassador McDowell, we meet again."

They exchanged a special handshake. "We've met before?"

"Very briefly, at the annual conclave held in the Bahamas. I was there with my father, Derrick, who's also here tonight."

"Derrick Eddington is here? That rascal." He turned to Pamela. "Honey, please excuse me for just a moment. I must go and say hello."

Jake spoke with a reserved TJ and an amused Brandon, and met their dates. Lincoln was forced to greet him as well. People were watching.

"It wasn't wise to come here," he said, managing to keep his face friendly. "You're throwing what you did to me right in my face."

"I'm here with my family, on behalf of my father and the Society of Ma'at, many of whom are in attendance tonight. My father was especially interested in reconnecting with Ambassador McDowell, and lending support to any causes of mutual interest. I'm also here with Sasha's godmother, Val, and yes, I'm here for Sasha. A man and his family among a thousand other guests. I'm sitting at my table. Sasha is sitting at yours. I am secure enough in who I am as a man to let this evening pass smoothly, with no further altercations of any kind. Are you?"

Instead of being the tense evening Jake had expected, the night proved to be the catalyst for positive change. By the end of the evening, the table occupants had shifted. Once dinner ended, the ambassador and Pamela joined Val at Jake's table. Ironically, a classmate of Ivy's, now an Atlanta councilman, was there, knew TJ well and wanted to introduce her to them.

She and Desmond sat in the seats Sasha's parents had vacated and maintained a cordial conversation. Jake watched as Cayden and Brandon conversed nearby. Reign joined Desmond and managed to briefly pull the style-conscious older Trotter sister, Millie, out of her shell. It was an evening of networking, hobnobbing and socializing. For Jake and Sasha, watching their families interact, and Lincoln eventually disappear into the crowd, it was definitely a night to remember.

"I can't believe this," Sasha whispered, as the evening wore down. "I didn't know how well your father knew my father."

"They're society, like myself."

Sasha was surprised. "You told me you never pledged."

"One doesn't pledge to join the Society of Ma'at. If they're lucky, one is chosen and then tested to make sure they are up to the task."

"That changes everything," she said, slightly in awe. "My mom will…never mind."

"Yeah, don't act like you're with me because of my status."

"No, baby," Sasha murmured, leaning into him. "I'm with you because of other, more arousing attributes."

They laughed as Jake led her out to the dance floor, making their official debut as a couple in front of the Trotters, the McDowells and everyone else.

Twenty-One

One year later

Beams of sun shimmered off the hundreds of silver tiles that had transformed a portion of the stunning grounds at Salamander, an upscale resort and spa nestled in the beautiful Virginian countryside an hour outside DC, into a tented outdoor sanctuary. Thousands of pearls and endless amounts of tulle adorned cushioned stainless steel chairs and paired seamlessly with the atrium where the pastor would stand to conduct the ceremony and Jake and Sasha would recite their vows. The guest list seamlessly blended the worlds of politics and sports, with a spattering of A-listers from stage, film and music. Ordinary folk were in attendance too. Friends from Sasha's Swiss boarding school and Brown, and Jake's buds from Northwestern University and Point du Sable. Everyone who'd ever meant anything to either of them, who'd helped to shape them into the adults in love that they were, had been invited to witness their special moment. Sasha's deep and abiding love for Jake had been enough to even cover Lincoln's transgressions. When his name showed up as a text on her phone as she sat for finishing touches on her makeup, she smiled instead of flinching.

I'll always wish the best for you. Hope Jake gives you a lifetime of happiness.

Sasha tagged the message with a heart. The threat of tears was unexpected.

"It took me thirty minutes to perfect that shadow combo," the makeup artist warned. "Don't!"

"I won't."

And she didn't. Just like she didn't mess up the endless ringlets the hair stylist had curled, or smudge her crystal-covered Jimmy Choo shoes or at any one time, either on her way to the altar or in the hours that followed, trip on the endless yards of pearl-and-crystal-covered silk, lace and organza that made up her one-of-a-kind gold-and-white wedding gown. The ball gown design boasted a chapel train with a sweetheart neckline, perfect for showing off the five-carat tear-drop yellow diamond that Jake had had delivered with that morning's egg white and spinach omelet. She was excited but maintained an unusual calm. Perhaps that's because Sasha knew with every fiber of her being that this moment was destined, even ordained. While not one who'd always dreamed of being married, Sasha was sure that her soul had known Jake was the one for her entire life.

Just as hair and makeup was completed, the dressing room door opened. In walked Reign, Sasha's maid of honor, and four of the nine bridesmaids. A verbal barrage ensued.

"You look amazing!"

"Wow, Sasha! What a gorgeous gown!"

"What a beautiful bride."

"Stunning! Fabulous!"

"Love your hair! Are those diamonds?"

"You're so pretty!"

"Geez! How long is that train?"

Reign held out a covered to-go cup. Her eyes shimmered with tears. "My brother's so lucky," she whispered. "Here, it's chamomile with lots of lemon and honey, to help calm your nerves."

"If that doesn't work," a bridesmaid interrupted while giving Sasha a hug from the other side. "I've got vodka."

The women stayed long enough to see Sasha corseted into all of her glory, glammed and gowned from head to toe. After a few selfies, hugs and words of encouragement they were shooed out the door by Avery and the On Point wedding team, a company Sasha now worked at part-time, and directed to take their places. Two attendants lifted the glittering gold-and-white eight-foot train as Sasha left the dressing room and entered the hall. Ambassador McDowell, tall and stately in a charcoal-gray tux, stood beaming and fighting tears.

"Today I give away a beautiful daughter," he whispered, his voice hoarse with a rare show of emotion. "But you'll always be my little girl."

Almost a thousand people stood in unison as Sasha and her father stopped in the center aisle at the back of the massive edifice. A quick scan revealed dozens of familiar faces but as she began the long walk from her past into her future, Sasha only saw Jake. She couldn't believe he was actually waiting there to become her one and only, couldn't imagine how she'd gotten so lucky as to have the man of her dreams now becoming her husband. Her heart skipped with pride as she glanced at the men standing with Jake to experience this moment. His brother, Desmond, as best man. His best friend, Cayden, wearing a satisfied smirk. Her brothers, TJ and Brandon, looking pleased and relaxed. Trenton, the pro basketball player Reign was dating who towered above them all. Still, his height of almost seven feet didn't detract from the center of her attention. The star in her heaven. The sun in her sky. Jake overshadowed them all. She hugged and kissed her father before offering an arm to her beloved. She turned and beheld a gaze with enough adoration to drown in. Enough to cause tears to gather and fall. Sasha dabbed them away and mentally recited her customized vows. The words that were stamped not only in her head, but also, and more importantly, in the depths of her heart.

Jake had to remember to breathe. Sasha's appearance sucked all the air out of the room. Her radiance dimmed the hanging chandeliers and obscured the rays of sunlight that streamed inside. She began walking toward him. His heart threatened to leap out of his chest.

Was this moment for real? Was this woman, so beautiful, so genuine, so intelligent, really getting ready to become his wife? The pastor broke through to answer Jake's question.

"We are gathered here today to join together this man and this woman in holy matrimony."

Sasha's voice was soft but certain. Jake's articulation could be felt in the soul. There were original poems and beautiful solos, but later Jake would most remember the most important part of the ceremony that mattered. When the pastor pronounced them man and wife and told Jake he could kiss his bride.

Once the ceremony ended, Jake and Sasha were whisked to a suite where the glam team helped Sasha trade her amazingly original yet cumbersome gold-and-white gown for an equally stunning fit-n-flare white sheath overlaid with an essence of gold tulle. She walked through the suite's connecting doors and into Jake's waiting arms.

"Baby, you look delectable." He moved his hands up and down her back. "The other dress was beautiful," he murmured against her earlobe. "But I like this one better."

He ran a finger along the hidden zipper.

Sasha laughed. "Oh, I get it. Easy access?"

"Exactly. In fact, can we skip the rest of the program and have a party of our own?"

Sasha shimmied away from his increasingly bold hands. "I think they'd miss us."

Jake pulled her back into his arms. "I don't care."

"You might not but with the work our moms, John

and the wedding coordinator put into that menu, I think it best we join them."

"Less than an hour in," Jake replied with a groan, "and marriage is already complicated."

Minutes after arriving downstairs, the emcee, a popular DC disc jockey, made the formal announcement. "Ladies and gentlemen, I present to you Mr. and Mrs. Jake and Sasha Eddington!"

They danced and hobnobbed, dined on Wagyu beef from Breedlove, Nevada, and lobster shipped fresh from Maine and downed it all with gallons of champagne from the award-winning vineyards at Drake Wines and Resort. Jake pulled the garter and Sasha threw the bouquet. Hours passed before the newly wed lovebirds were able to make their final rounds to bid quiet goodbyes to their families and close friends. Tomorrow, they'd board a private jet for a three-week honeymoon spanning the globe. Tonight, however, Jake and Sasha quietly slipped out a back entrance of the completely booked hotel filled solely with those who'd attended the wedding, and then headed to a lovely estate just up the road. It was owned by a sheik, its opulence at once grand and unapologetic. The couple oohed and aahed during a quick self-guided tour of the lavish surroundings, heady with champagne and lust and thoughts of forever. They kissed and cuddled in almost every room, with Jake reaching for the zipper on Sasha's third change of the day, a formfitting jumpsuit that he was happy to discover had nothing underneath it. He tried to unwrap his wedding gift before reaching the bedroom, but Sasha stilled his antsy hands, reiterating her desire to take a quick shower before they made their marriage official in every room and position they pleased.

After asking Jake to unzip the jumpsuit, Sasha reached for a small bag and headed for the en suite.

"I'll join you," Jake said, unbuttoning his shirt.

"Not this time," she replied with an impish smile. "Just get naked. I'll be quick."

Sasha didn't have to tell Jake twice. He stripped off his clothes, pulled back the spreads and tore the petals from a few nearby rose stems to strew on the bed. He spun the champagne chilling in a silver bucket around and placed it and two glasses on the nightstand for easy access. Climbing onto the king-size masterpiece, he lay back against the pillows and stared at the ceiling, listening to the sounds of water spraying in the room next door. Much like that first night, he imagined Sasha beneath the stream of water, her body wet and glistening, with tendrils of damp hair clinging to her baby-soft skin.

"Baby, what's taking you so long?"

"Almost ready," she playfully replied.

The bathroom door opened. Jake glanced up and saw a tail being swished back and forth. He sat up, his smile wide and knowing as Sasha came around the corner wearing a sexy tiger-striped nightie and a mask with ears.

"What's new, pussycat?" he asked, appreciative of the memory of their first night together.

"I'm looking for someone," she answered, climbing into bed. "His name is Zorro. Have you seen him?"

"Um, no. I don't think he's here."

Sasha pulled her hand from behind her back. It held

a black mask. "Well, you'd better find him and quickly. He's the one who I want to make love to me."

He eased the mask from her hand and pulled it over his eyes. "Zorro has just arrived," he said, before pulling her into his arms for a breathtaking kiss. Then he went about taking his pussycat from a game of secrets to one of seduction…that lasted all night long.

* * * * *

Get 4 FREE REWARDS!

We'll send you 2 FREE Books plus 2 FREE Mystery Gifts.

FREE Value Over $20

Both the **Harlequin® Desire** and **Harlequin Presents®** series feature compelling novels filled with passion, sensuality and intriguing scandals.

YES! Please send me 2 FREE novels from the Harlequin Desire or Harlequin Presents series and my 2 FREE gifts (gifts are worth about $10 retail). After receiving them, if I don't wish to receive any more books, I can return the shipping statement marked "cancel." If I don't cancel, I will receive 6 brand-new Harlequin Presents Larger-Print books every month and be billed just $6.30 each in the U.S. or $6.49 each in Canada, a savings of at least 10% off the cover price, or 6 Harlequin Desire books every month and be billed just $5.05 each in the U.S. or $5.74 each in Canada, a savings of at least 12% off the cover price. It's quite a bargain! Shipping and handling is just 50¢ per book in the U.S. and $1.25 per book in Canada.* I understand that accepting the 2 free books and gifts places me under no obligation to buy anything. I can always return a shipment and cancel at any time by calling the number below. The free books and gifts are mine to keep no matter what I decide.

Choose one: ☐ **Harlequin Desire**
(225/326 HDN GRJ7)

☐ **Harlequin Presents Larger-Print**
(176/376 HDN GRJ7)

Name (please print)

Address   Apt. #

City   State/Province   Zip/Postal Code

Email: Please check this box ☐ if you would like to receive newsletters and promotional emails from Harlequin Enterprises ULC and its affiliates. You can unsubscribe anytime.

Mail to the Harlequin Reader Service:
IN U.S.A.: P.O. Box 1341, Buffalo, NY 14240-8531
IN CANADA: P.O. Box 603, Fort Erie, Ontario L2A 5X3

Want to try 2 free books from another series? Call 1-800-873-8635 or visit www.ReaderService.com.

---

*Terms and prices subject to change without notice. Prices do not include sales taxes, which will be charged (if applicable) based on your state or country of residence. Canadian residents will be charged applicable taxes. Offer not valid in Quebec. This offer is limited to one order per household. Books received may not be as shown. Not valid for current subscribers to the Harlequin Presents or Harlequin Desire series. All orders subject to approval. Credit or debit balances in a customer's account(s) may be offset by any other outstanding balance owed by or to the customer. Please allow 4 to 6 weeks for delivery. Offer available while quantities last.

Your Privacy—Your information is being collected by Harlequin Enterprises ULC, operating as Harlequin Reader Service. For a complete summary of the information we collect, how we use this information and to whom it is disclosed, please visit our privacy notice located at corporate.harlequin.com/privacy-notice. From time to time we may also exchange your personal information with reputable third parties. If you wish to opt out of this sharing of your personal information, please visit readerservice.com/consumerschoice or call 1-800-873-8635. **Notice to California Residents**—Under California law, you have specific rights to control and access your data. For more information on these rights and how to exercise them, visit corporate.harlequin.com/california-privacy.

HDHP22R3

HARLEQUIN
PLUS

Announcing a **BRAND-NEW** multimedia subscription service for romance fans like you!

Read, Watch and Play.

Experience the easiest way to get the romance content you crave.

Start your **FREE 7 DAY TRIAL** at www.harlequinplus.com/freetrial.